P9-CSG-029

VALLEY OF THE HAWK

Although Corrie had always been very happy with her adoptive parents, when she learned that her real mother was alive and living in Ireland, she couldn't resist going over there to look for her. Her search led her not to her mother, but to Damon Courtney, a hard, impregnable man who immediately jumped to all the wrong conclusions about Corrie. That wouldn't have mattered much if she hadn't just as immediately fallen in love with him. But now she had two more problems: how could she get through Damon's distrust of all women—and what was she going to do about her fiancé John?

VALLEY OF THE HAWK

Margaret Mayo

ATLANTIC LARGE PRINT
Chivers Press, Bath, England.
John Curley & Associates Inc.,
South Yarmouth, Mass., USA.

Library of Congress Cataloging in Publication Data

Mayo, Margaret.
  Valley of the hawk.

  (Atlantic large print)
  1. Large type books.   I. Title.
  [PR6063.A93V3 1986]   823′.914   85–20705
  ISBN 0–89340–985–5 (Curley: lg. print)

British Library Cataloguing in Publication Data

Mayo, Margaret
  Valley of the hawk.—Large print ed.
  I. Title
  823′.914 [F]   PS35.A983

  ISBN 0–7451–9109–6

This Large Print edition is published by Chivers Press, England, and John Curley & Associates, Inc, U.S.A. 1986

Published by arrangement with Mills & Boon Limited

U.K. Hardback ISBN 0 7451 9109 6
U.S.A. Softback ISBN 0 89340 985 5

© Margaret Mayo 1980
Australian copyright 1980
Philippine copyright 1980

VALLEY OF THE HAWK

All the characters in this book have no existence outside the imagination of the Author, and have no relation whatsoever to anyone bearing the same name or names. They are not even distantly inspired by any individual known or unknown to the Author, and all the incidents are pure invention.

CHAPTER ONE

'I'm sorry, John, I can't go through with it.'

He looked stunned, the colour draining from his face. 'But, Corrie, why? Is it something I've done—or—' He frowned suddenly, 'is there someone else? Corrie, if there is, I'll wring his neck, I swear it.'

The girl shook her head sadly. 'There's no one else. It's just—well, something personal that's cropped up, and I can't marry you until I've—' She tailed off, unsure how to go on.

'You mean you're only postponing the wedding?' The look of relief on his face was plain. 'Why didn't you say so? I thought you meant—oh, to hell with what I thought,' and he pulled her into his arms, holding her close as if he never wanted to let her go.

Corrie turned her pale face away from his eager mouth, her wide eyes troubled, haunting shadows marring the creamy perfection of her skin. Her whole world felt as though it had been blown apart.

Insensitive for the moment to her inner torment John continued to embrace her, turning her face to his and kissing her lips, only letting her go when he received no response. 'Can't you tell me what's troubling you?' he asked harshly, thrusting his hands deep into his trouser pockets and scowling blackly. 'Why all the secrecy? If it's something personal surely I've a right to share it? After all, I shall be your husband soon—I hope—but I'm beginning to have doubts.'

Corrie looked up into his anxious brown eyes. Dear John, he wasn't particularly handsome, but he was good and kind—and reliable. She hated hurting him, but what else could she do? She couldn't marry him, not until she had got this thing clear in her own mind. 'You'll probably tell me I'm a fool, but I can't help it, John, I just have to find out, I really do.'

'Find out what, for Pete's sake? Quit stalling, Corrie, and tell me what's bugging you.'

Corrie twisted a strand of her long platinum hair round her fingers. 'A-Anne and David are not my real parents,' she said bluntly. She could no longer bring herself to say Mom and Dad, their revelation had hurt deeply, even though she knew that they had had only her best interests at heart.

'You mean you're adopted?' said John breezily. 'So what? Thousands of kids are. It doesn't make me love you any the less.' He laughed. 'If that's all that's bothering you, you silly goose, then you've nothing to worry

2

about. I don't mind, really I don't.'

'It's not quite as simple as that,' she said slowly. 'They—they never legally adopted me.'

'You mean your real parents could come along and claim you at any time?'

'I hardly think they're likely to do that,' said Corrie flatly, 'not after all this while. Besides, no one knows who my father was.'

'They weren't married?'

She shook her head. 'But I made Anne tell me about my real mother. She didn't want to, not at first, but when she could see I was determined she gave in. Apparently she was the sister of Anne's best friend and was only sixteen when she had me.'

'And she never tried to see you—or claim you back?'

'No, she left England after I was born.'

'Then I can't see what your problem is,' said John. 'It's all best forgotten.'

'But I have to find her, don't you see,' hissed Corrie. 'She's my own flesh and blood, she's all the family I have—now—and I want to see her.'

'Corrie,' John shook her by the shoulders, 'don't do this, you'll only hurt yourself. Think of Anne and David too, think of all the love and care they've unstintingly given you. Don't throw it all away, don't hurt them any more

3

than it must have done to tell you this. They've given their whole lives to you and they only told you the truth now because they love you and felt it right that you should know.'

'I can't help it.' Corrie shrugged herself free. 'It's something I must do. I shall never be happy until I've seen this thing through.'

John looked worried. 'You're stubborn, Corrie, I've never seen you like this before. Do Anne and David know what you plan to do?'

She nodded.

'And do they approve?'

'No, but they won't stand in my way, not like you're doing now.'

'Where does she live, this—this person you're so intent on finding?'

'Her last address was in Ireland, that was two years ago. I don't know whether she's still there, but I intend to find out.'

'I'll come with you,' he said decisively. 'I don't like the idea of you travelling alone.'

'No, John, I'm sorry, this is something *I* have to do. It's personal, I don't want you with me.'

He looked hurt. 'I think you'd better give this some real deep thought before you go rushing off. I'm going now, but I shall be back again tomorrow. I hope by then you'll have

4

come to your senses.'

He made no attempt to kiss her again, for which Corrie was thankful. In her present mood she did not feel like being fussed by anyone—not even John whom she loved very much.

Once he had gone she went up to her bedroom. She knew Anne and David would be waiting to hear what he had said, but somehow she could not face them, even though she knew that she was hurting them by her attitude. Why hadn't they told her before? she wondered. Why wait until now when she was making plans for her wedding?

She had been so happy. Only last week she and John had been looking at houses and had almost made up their minds to put a deposit on one of the new ones being built not far from where she lived in the Midlands town of Walsall. She had wanted to be near her parents, now she was not sure what she wanted any more—except to find her real mother. This was something she had to do, and no one, not even John, would dissuade her.

Corrie did not sleep well that night and by morning her mind was made up. She had two weeks' holiday due from the office, which she had intended using for her honeymoon, but she would take it now. Mr Higgins was an understanding man, if she told him she had personal problems he would be the first to agree that she must try and resolve them without delay.

She ate her breakfast, trying to ignore the worried look on Anne's face, realising her mother wanted to know whether she had changed her mind. It was all she could do to stop herself from throwing her arms round the older woman, saying, 'Please don't worry, I still love you, and I always shall, no matter what.' But she knew it was best not to, not at this stage. Once her plans were made then she would tell Anne, when there was no fear of her breaking down and being persuaded not to go through with it.

At the normal time she went out of the house, but she didn't go to the office, instead she phoned in, and as she had guessed Mr Higgins was agreeable to her taking her two weeks' holiday from that day.

Next she went to the travel agents and managed to make a reservation on the ferry from Fishguard to Rosslare that very same night. It was sooner than she had anticipated, but it was the only one available and she took it willingly.

Anne was surprised to see her back home again half way through the morning, and upset when Corrie told her of her plans.

'I'll come back, Mom,' Corrie said, 'don't worry, but this is something I have to do. Please understand.'

'I'm trying to,' said Anne tearfully, 'but how about John? What's he going to say?'

'He won't like it, he thinks I'm mad. It's probably best that I shall be gone before I see him again. He's coming round tonight, will you tell him for me?'

Anne nodded sadly. 'I wish I hadn't told you, but in one way it's a relief. It's been a burden all these years, wondering whether I was going to lose you. I hope it's not going to happen now, I don't think I could bear it.'

Corrie hugged her. 'I love you, Mom, and Dad too. I'll be back, never fear.'

She had gone then, feeling sad, as though it was the end of one chapter in her life and the beginning of another. But whereas before she had known where she was going, now she felt lost and for the first time began to wonder whether she was doing the right thing.

It was a long drive to Fishguard, but she could afford to take her time, almost letting her little red Mini find its own way while her thoughts were taken up with what lay ahead.

She had no clear idea what she would say when she saw her mother. Indeed she did not even know whether she would find her. There had been no news in over two years, so she could be anywhere in the world by now. It could well prove to be a fruitless journey, but at least she would have tried, that was the important thing.

It was in the early hours of the morning when the ferry arrived at Rosslare. Corrie had slept only intermittently, but she did not feel tired; indeed she was eager to be on her way.

Having previously bought a map of Ireland she discovered that the address she sought was in County Wicklow, about thirty or so miles away.

As she set off from Rosslare harbour a soft grey mist swirled about her car, changing to a magical pink as an unseen distant sun rose to herald the wakening of a new day. Gradually the mist cleared and Corrie caught her breath at the magnificent splendour of the surrounding countryside.

She stopped the car for a moment and climbed out, looking across the gently undulating hills. The fields and trees were lush and verdant—and it spelt peace. She breathed in deeply, for a few seconds able to forget the reason she was here. The Emerald Isle—how apt the name was, and what a contrast to the grimy town she had left behind.

Her journey took her through even more breathtaking countryside, deeply wooded valleys, cascading rivers and still lakes, and when she reached her destination she had the most peculiar feeling that she had come home, which was silly, for she had never been here before in her life. Her home was in England, with Anne and David, but something told her that she could settle down here—and be content. Perhaps that was why her mother had chosen Ireland? In this tranquil green land it would have been easy for her to forget her troubles—forget the unwanted child she had borne.

It was not difficult to find the address Anne had given to her. It was one of a row of tiny cottages in a village near Woodenbridge. It was still early, but smoke spiralled from the chimney and encouraged by this sign of life Corrie knocked on the door.

Her heart began to pound as she heard footsteps and she licked suddenly dry lips. The woman who appeared looked about the right age to be her mother and Corrie's heart sank. Whatever she had expected it had not been this. Her black, dyed hair was short and spiky and her over-bright eyes heavily ringed by lack of sleep. Thin lips slashed bright red across her face and her dress looked as though a wash would do it no harm. 'Yes?' she asked aggressively. 'What was it you would be wanting?'

Surely this was not her mother? Corrie felt like running away, the woman's unkempt appearance turned her stomach over. Anne had always been so clean and fastidious—to think that she might have been brought up by this awful woman! 'Mrs—Cunningham?' she asked slowly, 'Zelah Cunningham?'

To her tremendous relief the woman shook her head. 'She left here eighteen months ago,' and before Corrie could say anything else the door closed in her face, only to be opened again almost immediately. 'Why was it you were wanting her?'

'It's personal,' said Corrie politely but firmly. 'Did she leave a forwarding address? Do you know where I can find her?'

For the first time the woman looked closely at Corrie. 'Are you a relative or something?'

'Sort of.' Corrie did not wish to disclose her exact relationship, for this woman looked as though she was not averse to gossip. In no time at all the whole locality would know that she was looking for Zelah Cunningham—and no doubt they would put two and two together and come up with the right answer.

'My son might help you,' said the stranger suddenly, 'at least he can take you to someone who might know where she is now.'

Corrie missed the gleam in her eye, her main concern being that her task looked as though it might be easier than she had imagined.

But the young man who appeared when his mother called filled Corrie's heart with trepidation; he was a shifty-looking youth dressed in a manner as slovenly as the woman. He eyed Corrie with more than a hint of lust in his dark eyes and when his mother told him what was wanted he grinned and swaggered out of the house towards the parked Mini. 'Of course I'll help you, anything to oblige a lady.'

There seemed no way that she could get out of the situation, for he was already climbing into the car. Corrie bit her lip anxiously. Perhaps it would be all right, probably they were just being—helpful.

'It is but a few miles,' he said, as she started the engine. 'Turn round the way you've come and I'll show you.'

The lanes were narrow and there was no other traffic. Corrie felt nervous but tried not to show it, saying conversationally, 'This is beautiful countryside. You must be proud to live here.' The light wind chased clouds across the sky, dappling the fields and hedgerows in alternate shade and light. In the distance water glittered and far-away mountains were veiled in wreathing mist.

'To be sure I am,' he said, 'but it gets boring. There's no work, you see.'

11

'Then why don't you go to England or Europe and get a job?'

He shrugged and she guessed that he did not really want work.

'Is it far,' she asked next, 'to where Mrs Cunningham lives?'

'Zelah? My, but she was a beautiful lady. I was sorry when she left us.'

I bet you were, thought Corrie, disliking the way his face had lit up. Her apprehension increased for he had now turned in his seat and was regarding her with more than mere curiosity. When his hand moved to touch her hair she stiffened and drove just that little bit faster.

'Such beautiful hair,' he said, 'so silky and white, like Zelah's. I loved Zelah, you know. She never guessed, but I did. She used to let me brush her hair—and sometimes—'

He broke off and Corrie looked across at him. 'Sometimes you did what?' she asked, not at all sure she liked what he was saying.

'Sometimes—she would kiss me.' His breathing became erratic at the memories aroused and his hand slid down Corrie's shoulder, brushing her breast. 'You are like her,' he said harshly, his other hand reaching out to the handbrake and pulling it on.

'Stop it!' she cried, pushing her foot down harder on the accelerator and trying to knock

12

away his hand. The car careered across the road as they struggled and at the same time another car came in the opposite direction, the horn blaring loudly when the driver saw them approaching directly in his path.

Corrie slammed on her brakes and managed to stop a few inches away from the other vehicle. 'You nearly got us both killed!' she yelled furiously. 'If you lay your filthy hands on me again I'll—'

Her door was wrenched open and a strong male hand caught her arm, dragging her mercilessly from her seat. Outside the tall stranger still held her in a vice-like grip, pulling her slight form close to his powerful body. She could feel him taut with anger and as she tilted back her head to look up at him, he said, 'Next time you decide to have an argument with your boy-friend I suggest you stop the car first.'

Corrie's words of emphatic denial died on her lips as she encountered his dark eyes which blazed out of a strong, hawk-like face, his firm jaw tilted arrogantly. When she did not speak he shook her so violently that she was compelled to cling to him for support. 'Well, haven't you anything to say for yourself?' he asked harshly.

'For your information,' Corrie said tightly, 'he is not my boy-friend. He's—he was—

making a nuisance of himself. I was trying to stop him and that was when my car went out of control.'

'Then don't you think you ought to be more careful with whom you keep company?'

'He was merely showing me the way somewhere.' Corrie managed to wrench herself free. 'There's been no harm done, so I don't see why you're making so much fuss.' Standing back a pace, she was able to view him more clearly. Tall, lean, powerful, aged anywhere between thirty and forty. Good-looking in a rugged kind of way, but hard—hard as nails, she would say, judging by that ruthless expression in his grey eyes and the firming of his wide mouth. His jet-black hair had become windswept and he thrust impatient fingers through it now, at the same time scrutinising her face so intently that she began to feel nervous.

He lifted his shoulders. 'If that's your attitude I'll leave you to your fate, though my advice would be to continue your journey alone.'

Before Corrie could reply he had turned away and was now climbing back into his car. There had been no time to notice before, but now she observed that it was a silver-grey Rolls-Royce. No wonder he had been annoyed! She could just imagine his feelings if she had crashed into him in her old red Mini.

He reversed and then drove forward past her, without even so much as another glance. Corrie guessed he had pushed her completely out of his mind, dismissing her as nothing more than an incompetent woman driver.

To her amazement, when she climbed back into her own car the lad had disappeared. She had not seen him go, but during the time she was arguing with the driver of the Rolls anything could have happened and she would not have noticed. He had had that sort of effect on her. There was a powerful magnetism about him that would hold anyone's attention.

It was a relief to know that she would not have to put up with the boy's insolent manner, but it left her with no idea where to go in her continued search. Added to which she was uneasy about the way the boy had spoken. He made her mother sound—no, she refused to consider it, pushing these unwanted thoughts firmly from her mind.

She drove on, avoiding the potholes which cropped up with alarming frequency, but the further she went the more isolated her surroundings became. She passed through several small villages, but no one had heard of Zelah Cunningham and Corrie began to think that her journey was going to prove fruitless after all. She was reluctant to go back and enquire again, so she drove around becoming more and more frustrated as the day progressed.

The County of Wicklow had been described in her brochure as the Garden of Ireland and it was not difficult to see why, with such striking scenery. Masses of granite mountains frowned down on her and deep glens provided welcome shade from the heat of the sun, but she was really in no mood to appreciate her surroundings, anxious only to come to the end of her journey.

By late afternoon she decided she had better find somewhere to stay the night before it was too late, but first she posted the card Anne had insisted she send to let them know she had arrived safely.

She had no difficulty in finding a room in an attractive cottage overlooking a lake, and indeed felt that she could have spent several days here in this tranquil spot. But early the next morning she was off on her travels again, she could not afford to waste time indulging herself.

Systematically now she scoured the area, using her map to make sure she did not miss any of the small villages, certain that the place to which the boy had been bringing her could not be all that far away.

By afternoon she was tired and weary. She parked her car alongside a sandy beach and sat down on the low sea wall. It was lonely, this chasing around after someone who was no more than a name. She wished now that she had let John come with her, at least it would have relieved the monotony of her own company hour after hour.

At first she did not notice the group of teenagers who had come down on to the beach and were playing a vigorous game of baseball. It was not until the ball came in her direction and one of the young men came chasing after it that she really saw them.

'Hello there,' he called, 'you look lonely. Care to join us?'

Corrie shook her head. He looked a nice enough boy, far different from the disagreeable youth who had offered to show her the way yesterday. He had fair hair and a freshness about him that was appealing, but she had no desire to play games.

'Come on,' he persisted. 'We're having a barbecue later, it should be fun.'

Again she refused. 'No thanks. I'm after someone, name of Zelah Cunningham. Ever heard of her?'

'Sorry, but perhaps some of the others have.' He held out his hand. 'Let's go and ask.'

17

About to shake her head for a third time, a picture flashed before Corrie's mind's eye of the man in the Rolls. It was almost as though he was frowning down in disapproval—and that did it. 'Okay, I'll come,' she said, putting her hand into his and allowing him to pull her up from the wall.

They strolled across to the others who were shouting at him to hurry up with the ball. He made no attempt to let go her hand and Corrie did not resist. She had spent a lonely two days and was feeling more than a little sorry for herself.

Indeed she was doubting the wisdom of her self-imposed task and made up her mind that if she could still find no trace of her mother by tomorrow morning she would go back home and forget about the whole thing.

'What's your name?' asked the boy as they approached the rest of the crowd.

'Corrie,' she supplied willingly.

'And I'm Neil.'

He introduced her to the others who all seemed pleased to welcome her into their midst and for the next hour or so Corrie played a hilarious ball game, managing to forget for a while her reason for being here.

Later she helped gather driftwood and build the fire ready for their barbecue. She could not remember ever enjoying herself so much. As soon as darkness fell they lit the fire and cooked sausages and steaks and drank wine which they had in plentiful supply.

Afterwards one of the boys produced a guitar and they sang, sitting in a circle round the fire. Somehow, Corrie was not sure how it happened, the group split up into couples and she found herself alone with Neil, a little apart from the others, his arm firmly about her shoulders.

When he kissed her Corrie let him, it seemed only polite after the way they had included her in their party, but when his kisses became more possessive and he pulled her down on to the sand, one leg over her body so that she could not move, Corrie began to feel angry.

He was after all no different from any other boy she had met. It was her blonde hair that did it—they all thought she was easy game. Well, she was not—and when his hands began groping her body she begged him to stop.

He laughed and she could smell the alcohol on his breath, the reason for his present bravado. A quick glance across the sand revealed that everyone else had the same idea—the only difference being that the other girls were not resisting. It had probably been their intention all along to turn the whole affair into an all-night orgy—except that she

19

had been too stupid to realise it.

When it became plain that Neil was not taking any notice of her struggles she took the only course left open to her and bit his lip hard until she felt the salt taste of blood in her mouth.

With a strangled cry he let her go. 'You wildcat!' he exclaimed loudly, but Corrie hardly listened, she was busy scrambling to her feet and racing across the sand. Twice she fell, but she picked herself up, spitting sand from her mouth. When she realised she had left her shoes behind she faltered and looked back, but Neil was after her so there was nothing she could do but go without them.

Without looking where she was going Corrie set off again, crying out in alarm as she ran headlong into someone walking towards her. Two powerful arms caught and steadied her, an amused voice started to say, 'Hey, where are you—' changing tone abruptly when he saw who the girl was. 'Good lord, it's you! Having trouble with the boys again?'

The moon illuminated his face sufficiently for Corrie to see the hard lines of censure. His grey eyes looked like black smudges in the harsh contours of his face, his lips had thinned and his lean fingers dug painfully into her arm.

'So what if I am?' she replied hotly. 'It's no

business of yours.'

'Too true it isn't.' He let her go, looking thoughtfully back along the beach in the direction of the fire whose dying embers glowed like an angry red eye, giving just sufficient light to see the couples writhing on the sand. 'That the sort of thing you enjoy?' he asked abruptly.

'Would I be running away if it was?' Corrie glared up at the man who for the second time had appeared at the most inopportune moment.

'Then why get yourself involved in the first place? And don't try to tell me you didn't know what sort of party it was you got yourself invited to.'

Corrie shrugged, knowing he would only believe what he wanted, whatever she said. 'Think what you like, it makes no difference to me.'

'Where are your shoes?' he asked abruptly.

'Back there, but it doesn't matter, I have some more in my car.'

'Are you on holiday?' he asked next.

'Sort of,' admitted Corrie.

'Then if I were you I'd be careful as to the company I keep. A girl with your looks is asking for trouble.'

'Thanks for the warning. I'll go now before you conform to the pattern of the rest of your sex.' Her chin tilted defiantly, Corrie marched away from him with as much dignity as she could muster. It was difficult with bare feet, but she deliberately kept her back turned even though she was curious as to the reception her words had had. She knew he would not like her insinuation, but he deserved it. He was arrogant and pompous and she hated him.

In the few minutes it took to walk to her car Corrie tried to push him from her mind, but it was difficult, for with alarming persistence thoughts of him kept flooding back.

Although their two meetings had been brief she had a clear picture of him—the powerful, muscular body, the hidden lean strength beneath the superbly fitting clothes, and those keen eyes which missed nothing, framed as they were by thick dark lashes which were ridiculously long for a man.

She could still feel where his hands had held her arms and she rubbed them as if trying to eradicate the pain. For the moment the incident on the beach was forgotten. This man, this tall, good-looking stranger, had pushed everything else into the background. Why he should have this effect on her she was not sure, but he did, and she was angry with herself for allowing it to happen.

Corrie had walked a few hundred yards along the road before the horrified truth hit her. Her car had gone! Frantically she looked both ways. Perhaps she was in the wrong spot? But no, this was where she had left it, she knew that for sure.

She was walking up and down, almost crying in her distress, when a familiar voice said, 'Yours, I believe,' and the arrogant stranger held out her shoes.

It was not until he was close enough to hand them to her that he observed her anguish. 'What's the matter now?' he asked impatiently. 'Still crying over your foolish escapade?'

Corrie bent down and slipped on her shoes, too upset even to thank him for rescuing them. 'Someone's stolen my car.'

One thick dark brow rose questioningly. 'Are you sure?' he asked sardonically. 'You've been drinking, you could be mistaken.'

'And I'd be even more mistaken if I thought you would sympathise with me,' she snapped. 'Of course I know where I parked it, I haven't had that much.'

'Did you lock it?'

About to ask him what sort of a fool he thought she was, the sickening truth hit Corrie like a blow. She shook her head miserably. 'I don't think I did. I was sitting here on the wall, I didn't mean to leave it.'

'I suppose you left your keys in the ignition

23

as well?' he drawled.

He clearly thought her all sorts of an idiot and Corrie knew she deserved it. 'Yes,' she said, in a small thin voice. 'My handbag was in it too—and my suitcase. They've all gone. What am I going to do?'

CHAPTER TWO

For several long seconds there was silence between them. Corrie had never felt more distraught, nor so much a fool, and judging by the expression on her companion's face his thoughts were running along very much the same lines.

'I would never have believed anyone could be so idiotic,' he said at length. 'Talk about dumb blondes—there's certainly truth in the saying.'

'It wasn't my fault,' defended Corrie crossly. 'If that boy hadn't asked me to join them none of this would have happened.'

'So—' he mocked, his lips curled in derisive amusement, 'it's the boy's fault that you left your car unlocked, with your money in it— *and* the keys. How amazing!'

She turned away in despair. 'I might have known you wouldn't understand. Thanks for finding my shoes, and *goodbye*.' She walked away, frantically trying to decide what to do next. The police were her best bet, but where in this out-of-the-way place would she find a police station? She couldn't recall seeing one since she'd landed in Ireland.

His footsteps behind her made her increase her pace. He was the last person she would turn to for help.

'Where are you staying?' His voice came over her shoulder. 'Perhaps I can help?'

A surprising offer coming from him, but Corrie did not alter her pace. 'I'm—I'm travelling around.'

She heard his exasperated sigh. 'Spare me from brainless females!' He caught up with her and shortened his stride so that he kept abreast. 'You mean you've nowhere to go tonight? What kind of a damn fool are you?'

What could she say? He regarded her as completely irresponsible already, so there was no point in trying to defend herself. She knew she had never done anything so stupid before, but he didn't—and he obviously saw her as one of those women who go through life with a couldn't-care-less attitude, causing chaos wherever they go. So she maintained a stubborn silence, walking along at his side, acutely aware of his stature and wishing that she herself had a few more inches so that she did not feel so dwarfed by his dominating presence.

When she did not answer he said, 'I can guess what you're up to, your type are all the same. What sort of a guy were you hoping to find?'

Without stopping to think Corrie swung her arm round in an arc, intending to strike him for the insult, but he was quicker than she, anticipating her action and catching her arm. It was wrenched behind her and she was imprisoned at his side.

Again, as yesterday, she felt the power in his limbs and an unfamiliar thrill coursed through her veins. There was something about this man that was dangerously attractive and for just a second she wondered what it would be like to be kissed by him.

Then the moment passed and she was struggling to free herself. 'I did come here to find someone,' she cried, 'but it was certainly not a fellow. In case you're interested, I already have a boy-friend.'

'So what's he doing letting you wander about Ireland on your own? He can't think much of you. I mean—' he looked her up and down with an insolence that made Corrie draw in her breath in anger, 'a girl like you is an open target.'

'What do you mean, a girl like me?' she

gasped furiously.

'A dyed blonde. Why does a girl do it, unless she wants to attract attention to herself?'

'My hair is its natural colour,' she defended hotly, tossing her head so that its silky platinum length swung about her shoulders. Many times she had been asked if she dyed it, but never with the rudeness of this man now. 'And will you let go my arm, you're hurting!'

He pulled her round to face him, his eyes probing deep into her own, his features an expressionless mask so that she had no idea what he was thinking. Then he released her with an abruptness that almost caused her to fall backwards. 'The question remains, where are you going to sleep tonight?'

'Oh, don't worry about me,' Corrie flung back haughtily, 'I shall find somewhere. Don't upset yourself on my behalf.'

'I shan't do that, never fear, but I do have a conscience and I shouldn't sleep easy in my bed if I thought you were roaming the roads of Ireland all by your pretty self.'

He mocked her, she knew, but nevertheless she could not resist a heated reply. 'Then what do you suggest, that I come home with you?'

'There seems little alternative.'

His voice was deceptively mild and Corrie stared at him aghast. 'You're not serious?'

27

'Unfortunately, yes, unless you can think of anything better?'

Their eyes met and locked—Corrie's wide and apprehensive, his cool and distant. He was certainly not making this offer out of the kindness of his heart, she thought. Pity perhaps, or contempt for her stupidity, but not because he was in any way attracted to her. She would certainly be safe in that respect. 'As you say, I don't have much choice, but I don't like the idea.' The thought of being in any way obligated to him was as much abhorrent to her as the idea of her staying in his house was to him.

'That makes two of us, but now we've decided on our course of action there's not much point in hanging about. Hawksmoor's about two miles from here, think you can make it?'

Corrie frowned. 'I don't know what sort of opinion it is you have of me, Mr Whatever-your-name-is, but I can assure you that I have a perfectly good pair of legs and walking happens to be one of the pleasures I enjoy.'

'Good, I'm glad to hear it,' and he set off, leaving Corrie to follow. She was compelled to trot to keep up with his long strides and they had gone several hundred yards before he appeared to notice. He slowed and she was able to catch her breath, but he did not speak.

Indeed his whole attitude was one of controlled impatience. He was not failing to make it clear that he did not like this idea, only a sense of moral responsibility had led him to it.

She herself was in no position to refuse. With no money and no transport she was in a very tricky situation and for the moment it might be best to ignore his ill-humour and accept his offer of help, much as she would like to tell him what he could do with it.

When Corrie had said she enjoyed walking, she meant it, but she had not realised that these two miles were uphill for most of the way, the lane becoming narrower all the time until it was virtually no more than a track wide enough for one car. Once or twice she stumbled, but her companion gave no indication that he noticed, striding along with his hands thrust deeply into his trouser pockets, not even bothering to speak, almost as though he had forgotten her presence.

'You don't have to do this,' she ventured. 'There must be somewhere else I can go without putting you to any trouble.'

'If there was I would have suggested it,' he said tersely. 'Save your breath for the rest of the journey, you'll need it.'

She shrugged and trudged on. The word Hawksmoor intrigued her. It sounded a wild

29

desolate place and she wondered whether it was the name of his house or perhaps a village. No doubt she would find out soon enough, but meanwhile she conjured up pictures of the sort of place it would be—anything from a huge black country mansion standing in splendid isolation to a cluster of tiny cottages nestling against the hillside.

Soon she had no energy left to even think, the path wound steeply upwards and her protesting legs felt as though they would never make it. On the other hand the stranger never altered his pace, the shadowy outline of his body sometimes disappearing altogether through the trees that grew more thickly the higher they climbed. The path had narrowed until it was no more than a single file track and it occurred to her that there must be more than one way to his house, for there was no way that a vehicle could make it.

When suddenly they emerged into a clearing Corrie stopped. The pale light of the silvery moon spilled down on to a house that at first looked little more than a ruin and for a few heart-stopping seconds she wondered where it was that he had brought her, and what it was she had let herself in for.

As she began to walk slowly nearer across the springy turf she could see scaffolding against the walls and piles of bricks as well as heaps of sand and gravel. 'Is this where you live?' she asked, running to catch up with him.

At closer quarters she could see that part of the roof was also missing and she felt an urge to turn about and go back the way she had come. He had to be joking; he couldn't live here, not in this derelict stone building. It had been beautiful once, she could see that; a huge manor house that would probably have housed a large family, but it must have been empty for many years for it to have fallen into this state.

'Are you having second thoughts?' He paused and looked down on to her face pale with moonshine. She did not know that she looked a frail colourless shadow, her hair and dress losing what little colour they had. In contrast the stranger, dressed all in black, was a solid, somehow menacing figure, and she shivered as she looked up at him, the chiselled planes of his face the only parts that were clearly visible.

'It looks—empty,' she said in a frail voice. 'Surely it's not fit to live in?'

'Beggars can't be choosers,' he said. 'If you want a roof over your head you'll have to put up with it.'

A roof over her head! Half a roof, he meant. All she could hope was the inside was better.

What she could not understand was why he should live somewhere like this yet at the same time own a brand new Rolls-Royce. It did not make sense.

Her heart thumped painfully as she followed him the last few yards, their feet echoing across a cobbled yard. A rotting wooden door opened beneath his hand and she groped her way along a narrow passage, wanting to reach out and touch the man in front of her, to use him as her guide, but knowing that he would shake himself free if she even so much as attempted it.

When he stopped she almost collided into him, but the next instant he had opened a door, switching on a light simultaneously so that its yellow glow spilled out into the corridor.

He turned as she stepped forward into the room. For the first time that night she saw his face clearly and almost wished it was still dark. At least then she would not have been so vividly aware of the grimness of his lips or the flintlike hardness of his dark eyes as he looked down at her. He made her feel as though she was a stray he had dragged in out of the street.

'I appreciate what you're doing for me,' she said hesitantly. 'I—I'll pay you back, as soon as I can.'

Still the unwavering steel eyes looked down

32

on her, rooting her to the spot. 'You can work for your keep.' His voice was as hard as his eyes. 'We find it difficult to keep staff while the house is in its present condition. You can start by putting on the kettle and making me a cup of coffee. I'll be back in a moment.'

He disappeared through another door and Corrie stared after him, wondering a few seconds later why she had not objected. Why she had let him give orders without declaring that that was not the reason she had come and if he wanted a drink he could make it himself. 'We,' he had said. Was he married? If so the woman must be a fool to get herself tied to someone as detestable as him.

Sighing, she looked about her. The kitchen was surprisingly in good order. The stone walls were white-washed and a dresser and cupboards in natural wood were obviously new additions. There was even a washing machine and a tumble-dryer, as well as a deep-freeze and a dishwasher. Yet he could still get no one to work for him! It was the man himself, she decided, not the conditions. It was his overpowering air of authority. Anyone would object to being ordered about the way he did. Not so much as a please or thank you, just, 'Make my coffee.' He probably demanded love of his wife in much the same way.

Corrie worked herself up into quite a fury thinking about it and was still standing where he had left her when he returned. He frowned. 'Are you incapable as well as incredibly stupid?'

She tilted her chin in a defiant gesture. 'I don't see why I should let you order me about. If you want a drink make it yourself, and if you'll show me where I'm going to sleep I'll get out of your way.'

His eyes narrowed, nostrils flaring. He strode across the kitchen and flung open the door. 'The sky can be your roof and the grass your bed. Goodnight to you, miss.'

Corrie took a step forward, then paused. She would be a fool to throw away the chance of a comfortable bed just because she felt insulted. Besides, she could do with a drink herself, the long walk had brought on a thirst.

As if reading her thoughts he said, 'If you've had a change of heart the kettle's over there.'

Biting back an angry retort, Corrie moved towards it. She removed the lid and held it under the tap. The water came out in peculiar little bursts, but at last it was full and she replaced the lid, plugging the kettle into the socket and switching on, all the time aware that she was being watched. Trying to ignore his intent regard, she gathered up cups and

34

saucers from the dresser, found coffee and sugar in canisters nearby and milk from the fridge.

'Make it three,' he said, as she spooned coffee into two cups only.

Corrie obeyed but maintained her silence, which was easy enough while she was occupied, but once the cups were ready and there was nothing to do but wait for the water to boil, it became embarrassing standing there, knowing he still had not moved his eyes from her face.

'What's your name?' he asked at length, his deep voice booming into the silence with a suddenness that made her jump.

'Corrie Maitland,' she said stiffly. 'What's yours?'

'Courtney, Damon Courtney,' came the ready response. 'You said you were on a *type* of holiday. What did you mean?'

'I don't see that it's any business of yours,' she began heatedly, when she realised that maybe here was someone who could help her. He seemed the sort of man who would know plenty of people. 'But if you're really interested, I'm looking for someone. Perhaps you know her? She has an unusual name— Zelah Cunningham—one that you might remember?'

The harsh lines on his face deepened. 'Oh,

yes,' he said, 'I would remember all right.' His voice so cold it was frightening, but Corrie was scarcely aware of it. At last she had found someone who knew her mother. If only she had thought to ask him the first time they met it would have saved all this trouble.

'But you're wasting your time, she's no longer in Ireland and I doubt she will return. Why did you want her?'

Corrie felt deflated. Her hopes which had risen so quickly had been burst like a balloon. 'It doesn't matter,' she said wearily, 'not if she's gone.' Then on a note of hope, 'You don't happen to know where she is now?'

'Zelah never stays in one place for very long,' he said, 'which you'll realise if you know anything at all about her. You haven't answered my question. Why are you trying to find her?'

She shrugged. 'It's not important.'

'But it must be,' he persisted, 'if it's brought you over here. Where do you come from—England?' and as she nodded, 'It's my guess you're a relative.'

'Why do you say that?' asked Corrie quickly.

'I think you must know,' he said, 'but I'd rather not discuss her any more if you don't mind. I find the subject distasteful.'

Corrie though, her appetite now whetted,

36

asked, 'Did you know her personally?'

'Oh, yes.'

And the way he said it, and the way his eyes glittered and his mouth thinned, made Corrie aware that Zelah was not a woman he liked. Had there been anything going between them at one time? They must both be roughly the same age. What a coincidence that she had bumped into someone who actually knew her! 'What was she like?' she asked eagerly, almost before she realised it.

He snorted with derision. 'Like all women, out for what she could get. The kettle's boiling.'

As she made the coffee Corrie realised that the subject was closed, but only for the time being, because she did not intend leaving this house without finding out much more concerning this woman who was her mother.

He might not like her, and it hurt, what he had said—spoiled the mental image she had built up—but after all, Zelah was her own flesh and blood and maybe he had a thing about women anyway. It sounded like it.

He took the third cup and saucer out of the room but returned a few moments later. Corrie had sat down at the table in the centre of the kitchen, expecting him to do likewise, but instead he took his cup and leaned back against the door, once again eyeing her in that

37

disconcerting manner he had. 'If you're worrying about how you're going to get back home with no money, I'll fly you. I was going over there later in the week anyway, so I may as well go tomorrow.'

Corrie did not like the way he was taking over, even though he was in his own way helping her out. She said, 'How about my car? I can't go without doing something about that.'

'Leave it to me,' he said. 'If it should turn up I'll get it shipped over.'

'How kind of you,' Corrie returned sarcastically. 'Anything, I suppose, to get me out of your way. What are you afraid of, that if I remain over here I'll turn up on your doorstep again like a bad penny?'

'Nothing of the kind,' he said crossly, 'but what's to keep you now that your search has proved unsuccessful? I thought you'd jump at the chance of a free lift home. Not many people in your position would find themselves so fortunate.'

'I don't flatter myself that you're doing it out of kindness!'

'I'm not,' he said aggravatingly, 'but I don't think you have any choice. You either accept my help or take the consequences. Even if you find your car it's doubtful whether your purse will still be in it, so what will you do then?'

'I can phone my parents and ask them to transfer some money from my bank account.'

'It's Sunday tomorrow,' he said. 'Even if the bank can fix it up on Monday it will be Tuesday at least before you can draw any. That's nearly four days you have to exist.'

Corrie didn't know why she was arguing. He was right, there really was no point in her remaining here any longer. Her only excuse was that it was a beautiful country and she would like to spend a few days holidaying here. It seemed a pity to make the journey and then return before she had seen anything of the island. But without money, what could she do? 'I suppose you're right,' she said at last, setting her cup in its saucer.

Almost as if he had been waiting for her to finish he pushed himself away from the door, nodding in a satisfied sort of way. 'If you're ready I'll show you where you can sleep. It's nothing fancy, but we weren't expecting visitors.'

The stairs led directly from the kitchen through a door she had not noticed before. There was no light and Corrie stumbled up behind him in the darkness, shuddering a little, finding the whole atmosphere of the house far from restful.

They turned sharply at the top of the stairs, almost doubling back on themselves, and

Damon Courtney opened a door. She followed him inside, waiting for him to press the switch, shocked when he said, 'I'm afraid there's no light. Only the main rooms are wired so far.' He crossed to the window, rubbing his fingertips across the grimy panes. 'The moon's still shining. You should be able to see to undress.'

Before she could protest he had gone, the door closing with a definite click and his feet echoing down the carpetless stairs.

Corrie was scared, not of the man, but the room. How did she know the bed was clean? It was difficult to see, but if the dirt on the windows was anything to go by, it didn't say much for the rest of the room.

She struggled with the catch and managed to fling it open wide, allowing the light of the moon to beam in now with sudden clarity. The bed was made up—and it looked clean. Perhaps she was doing him an injustice? But even so she did not undress, sliding between the sheets fully clothed.

Having slept little the previous two nights she expected to fall asleep immediately, but instead found her thoughts dwelling on Damon Courtney. After his initial hostility he had surprised her by offering help, but now she could see why. Perhaps he had thought to humiliate her by bringing her here, or had it

40

been in his mind to get some unpaid assistance? Had she known she would have refused to come, but despite his arrogance there was something about him that fascinated her. He was unlike any other man she had met, and there had been plenty of those, but until she met John she had been serious about none.

For the first time for many hours her thoughts dwelled on John and she felt faintly amused that he had been pushed completely out of her mind. 'I'm sorry, John,' she whispered, 'if I let you come with me none of this would have happened.' He would be surprised to see her back home tomorrow, surprised and pleased. She did not want to go but really could not afford to turn down Damon Courtney's offer.

As sleep claimed her Corrie's last vision was of Damon Courtney's disturbing face and she could not help but wonder once again what it would be like to be kissed by him, to have those generously moulded lips pressed on hers, and those strong arms wrapped about her in passion rather than anger.

Immediately the thoughts entered her mind she banished them, feeling an enormous sense of guilt. Whatever was she thinking? How could she let down John in such a manner? But all the same Damon Courtney's face continued to haunt her as she fell asleep.

CHAPTER THREE

When Corrie woke she could not for a moment remember where she was. She looked at the walls where the paper had once been a pretty pink sprigged with wild flowers, but which now was sullied by brown damp patches, and the flaking ceiling was a dirty grey instead of white. There were no curtains at the windows, but one of them was open and she suddenly recalled the events of last night.

Despite its dingy appearance the room itself was clean. A threadbare rug covered the boarded floor, a marble-topped table held a pitcher of water and a bowl, and a towel was folded neatly over the back of a chair. But the bed was new, and the sheets and covers, looking incongruously out of place in their shabby surroundings.

She washed her hands and face and combed her hair with her fingers as best she could, smoothing down her cotton dress which had inevitably become creased. She wished now that she had taken it off. Had she known how beautifully clean the bed was she would not have hesitated.

Her watch had stopped so she had no idea what time it was, but as she made her way downstairs she could hear movements in the kitchen below. Someone was up. Was it Damon Courtney—or his wife—or perhaps both? But when she pushed open the door it was neither. The man who turned to look at her in astonishment was aged about sixty, although he could be older. He had the same hawk-like features as Damon Courtney, but his eyes were a piercing blue and his hair had turned to a steely-grey. He was as tall and erect as Damon and Corrie had no difficulty in guessing that this was his father.

She was not prepared, though, for the effect that her appearance had on him. The colour drained from his face and he clutched the table for support. 'Who are you?' he asked hoarsely. 'What are you doing here?'

'I'm sorry if I startled you,' she said. 'My name's Corrie Maitland. Hasn't your son told you, my car was stolen last night and he kindly offered to put me up.'

'Oh, yes,' said the old man vaguely, 'he did say something about inviting someone back here. I rather thought it was another man, I don't know why.'

He had phrased it politely, thought Corrie, if that was what he had said. Invited! An offer begrudgingly given would have been more

43

like it.

'Forgive me if I stared,' continued Mr Courtney, 'but you—you—remind me of someone.'

Corrie nodded. 'Zelah? Yes, I'm beginning to realise that I must look a bit like her. I'm sorry, I don't know how well you knew her, but I've gathered from your son that she didn't make a very good impression?'

'Not so far as he was concerned,' he replied sadly. The colour had returned to his cheeks and he was once again in full control of himself. 'I apologise if I appeared rude. I expect you'd like some breakfast. I'm just going to cook myself ham and eggs, how does that sound?'

'Super,' agreed Corrie at once. She had eaten only sketchy meals yesterday and suddenly realised how hungry she was. 'Can I help?'

'Sit and talk to me,' he said. 'It's not often we have female company in this house. You're like a breath of spring.'

Corrie could not help asking, 'Is Damon married?'

His father snorted. 'He's a woman-hater, in case you hadn't realised. To tell you the truth I'm surprised he brought you here.'

'So am I,' confirmed Corrie, 'but I think he only did it out of a sense of moral obligation.'

'That sounds like my son,' he agreed, laying two slices of ham into a huge cast iron frying pan which he carried across to the stove. 'He might not like women, but he would never fail to help anyone in trouble. Had your car stolen, you say? Bad luck that, how did it happen?'

Corrie bit her lip. 'It was my fault really, I left my keys in. I'm not usually so stupid, but—well, I was a bit fed up, so I suppose it made me absentminded. My money was in it as well, did Damon tell you that?'

His father shook his head. 'You really are in a state, but I'm sure it will turn out right in the end.' He looked at her creased dress. 'There's some clothes upstairs, if you want to help yourself. They were—my wife's, but they should fit you, you're about the same size.'

'Thank you, Mr Courtney.' Corrie doubted whether they would be her style, but at least they would be clean and fresh. She was miserably aware of the sight she must look. 'And have you a comb or brush I could borrow? I must look terrible!'

'You could never look that, my dear child, and call me Charles, we don't stand on ceremony here. If you'd like to change now, while I'm cooking breakfast? Damon's out, so there'll be no one to bother you.'

Corrie nodded eagerly. 'If you'd just tell me where to go. It was dark when I arrived last night.'

'And the whole place looked a shambles? I know, but we're knocking it into shape bit by bit. You'll have to excuse us, I'm afraid, if it's not quite what you're accustomed to.'

'Oh, it's not that.' Corrie would hate him to think that she was criticising. 'It's just that Damon didn't bother to explain. He took me up to that room—and I thought—'

'Ah, I see,' he cut in. 'I wondered what you were doing coming through that door. I'm afraid my son was playing a trick on you. That's part of the house that hasn't yet been restored. We keep a bed made up for emergencies, but there was no need for Damon to put you there. I'll have a word with him when he comes in.'

'Don't do that,' said Corrie at once. 'If he thought I'd been complaining, well, he doesn't think much of me already, and I don't particularly want to make matters worse, not if he's taking me back to England today.' For some reason that even she herself did not know she did not want his opinion of her to drop any lower.

Charles nodded, as if he understood, though Corrie was sure he could not. He moved the frying pan so that the ham would not burn and said, 'Come along. I'll show you how the whole house will look eventually. It's such a pity it's been left to decay and I can't wait to see it all restored.'

They went through the door where Damon had taken the coffee last night. It led into a corridor whose floor was magnificently tiled in Italian marble. At the end a flight of stairs carpeted in rich dark red led to a long landing.

'Here we are,' said Charles, 'this was my wife's dressing room. Take your pick, you can have a bath too, if you like. You'll find everything you need.'

Corrie hesitated once she was alone, feeling somehow reluctant at the thought of wearing a dead woman's clothes, but when she opened the wardrobe and saw the beautiful array of dresses all her fears disappeared. They were surprisingly modern, almost the sort of clothes she would wear herself. It puzzled her and the only explanation she could think was that his wife must have been much younger than himself.

The bathroom was a dream in pink and gold and Corrie would have loved a long scented bath, but she compromised with a shower, washing her hair also when she saw that there was an electric dryer.

In half an hour she was ready to return downstairs. The dress she had chosen was in cornflower blue jersey, clinging to her sylph-like figure, adding to her natural grace. She had toyed with the idea of fastening her hair up, but she always liked it when it was freshly shampooed, so she let it fall in its natural silken waves.

Charles' eyes narrowed when he looked at her as she re-entered the kitchen, but otherwise gave no indication that he recognised the dress.

'Thank you,' said Corrie shyly. 'I feel much better.'

The table was laid and breakfast ready. They sat down and Charles poured coffee. 'Tell me about yourself,' he said. 'What are you doing in Ireland alone?'

'I'm on holiday,' she said. It was partially correct and somehow she felt reluctant to tell him the truth. Zelah Cunningham did not appear to be a very welcome name in this household and she could find out all she wanted from Damon on the way home. 'I was hoping to tour the whole of Ireland, but I guess that's finished. It's very good of your son to offer to fly me back. I don't know what I'd have done otherwise, with no money or anything.'

'Mm.' Charles looked thoughtful. 'Why did you choose to holiday alone? Have you no family, or friends, who would have come with

48

you? It seems strange to me that a girl as pretty as you should prefer her own company.'

'It was my choice,' said Corrie. 'John, that's my fiancé, he wanted to come, but I wouldn't let him, and my parents—well, they knew I wanted to be alone.'

'Having a last fling before you get married, eh?' he laughed.

'Something like that,' she agreed.

'And what sort of work do you do? Are you a model? You have the—' He searched for the right word, trying to express himself with his hands.

Corrie laughed. 'I work in an office— shorthand, typing, book-keeping, anything that needs doing. You know the sort of thing.'

'Indeed I do.' He sounded enthusiastic. 'And do you like your work? I mean, shall you be sorry to leave when you get married?'

Corrie cut a neat slice of ham and chewed on it thoughtfully before answering. Married to John! It was strange, but all that seemed so far away now and yet it was only three days since she had left for Ireland. It seemed a lifetime. She supposed she ought to be looking forward to going back, but when she looked at the man opposite she saw in his place a younger version with rich black hair and ruthless lips—and deep stormy eyes which

49

blazed into her very soul. And she knew that she wanted to remain here a while longer. It was ridiculous after the way he had treated her, but there was a charisma about him, a fatal fascination that drew her as surely as a moth to a flame, and she wanted to find out more about this man who had brought her to his house in the dark of night.

'You haven't answered my question,' Charles nudged gently. 'I swear you've been staring at me for a full five minutes.'

'Sorry,' she laughed. 'You set my mind working. No, I don't think I shall mind leaving. I love the work, of course, but I can't see myself as a career woman.'

Again he looked thoughtful. 'I see you wear no ring. Is there nothing definite between you and your young man?'

'We decided it was a waste of money,' she admitted. 'We'd rather put it towards a house.' In fact it had been John's suggestion, but somehow it had not seemed to bother her. She wondered why Charles was asking all these questions—not that she minded, she quite enjoyed talking to him. He was a charming gentleman and had certainly a much more agreeable nature than his son. But his next question shook her.

'How would you like to work for me?'

He smiled at her shock, continuing, 'Let

50

me explain. I'm attempting to write the history of this house. It's been in our family for hundreds of years, but Damon and I knew nothing about it until a few years ago when we discovered that we'd inherited Hawksmoor. We lived in England at the time and never even knew that we had Irish ancestors. You'll learn the whole story if you agree to help me, it's totally fascinating.'

'What is it you would want me to do?' asked Corrie, still bemused.

'All the paper work,' he said. 'I'm hopeless when it comes to that. My study's a shambles, but if you could put it all into some sort of order and type out the facts so far it would be a tremendous help. I'm sure you'll soon become as completely absorbed in it as I am myself.'

He was so enthusiastic Corrie could not help feeling excited. 'I will,' she said, her mind suddenly made up. 'I'd like it. Thank you very much, Charles.'

Goodness knows what they would say at home when they found out, and she would not admit, even to herself, that it was perhaps the son, not the father, who was the attraction. But when he leaned across the table to drop a kiss on her forehead she could not help lifting her face and returning his kiss. He really was a dear.

If Corrie could have chosen a moment for Damon to return it would certainly not have been that one. The door opened at the precise moment she was kissing his father, and Damon, who had been smiling happily when he entered the kitchen, stopped, his face changing dramatically.

For one moment he looked as though he could hardly believe his eyes, his thick brows drew together in a heavy frown and there was a tenseness about his jaw that told Corrie how angry he was. With one violent movement he kicked the door shut so that the sound reverberated round the room.

His father looked at him in mild surprise, but it was Damon who spoke first. 'Good morning, Father. I see you and Miss Maitland are already—well acquainted. I never thought she'd get up to her tricks with you.'

Charles looked puzzled. 'What do you mean? This young lady and I are getting on famously.'

'I can see that,' scoffed Damon. 'But wouldn't you say you were being a little too friendly on such a short acquaintance? Perhaps I ought to warn you before it's too late exactly what sort of a person Miss Maitland is.' He stalked round to the other side of the table and sat down, his cold granite eyes firmly fixed on Corrie.

She stared haughtily back. 'I think, Mr Courtney, you ought to be careful what you're saying. I can sue you for defamation of character.'

'But you wouldn't,' he said, with a smile that meant nothing. 'Because it would be your word against mine, and we both know who would win.'

'Damon!' admonished his father. 'I don't know what this is all about, but I'm sure I'm not going to have a guest in our house spoken to in this manner. I thought you only met her yesterday, so what has she done to make you so much against her?'

'Nothing,' put in Corrie quickly. 'He's made up his mind what sort of a person I am for no reason at all. Your son is a very doubting person.'

'Not without just cause,' Damon retorted. 'Perhaps, Father, you won't be so trusting if I tell you that last night was not the first time I had met Corrie—and both times there was a boy involved. The first time she was trying to fight off his advances and nearly crashed into my car. The second time she was running away from a beach orgy in which she'd got herself involved.' He paused, waiting for his words to take effect. 'Now do you see what she's like? I was disgusted when I saw her kissing you. How could she? And how could you, Father?'

Corrie was about to speak when Charles halted her with a lift of his hand. 'Damon, why do you never wait for explanations? Why do you always draw your own conclusions? I'm sure Miss Maitland has some perfectly logical reason for her actions.'

A muscle worked in Damon's jaw as he strove to control his anger. 'Trust you to champion her, Father! I think we both know why that is, though it would appear that Miss Maitland herself is ignorant of the fact. Why don't you tell her?'

'I don't see the necessity,' said Charles Courtney. 'Not yet, anyway. Perhaps later.'

Puzzled as to what they could be talking about, Corrie looked from one to the other, but she was given no opportunity to speak.

'There'll be no time later, I'm flying Corrie back to England today. That's where I've been this morning, making certain that my plane will be ready.'

Corrie thought she saw a twinkle in the older man's eye, but she could not be sure, for when he spoke his face was perfectly serious. 'There's no need for that now, my son. Corrie is staying.'

'For how long?' exploded Damon. 'My God, she's a fast worker! I never dreamt anything like this would happen before I got

54

back.' He looked at Corrie, his mouth drawn into a grim line and his eyes as coldly furious as they could be.

She shivered beneath the onslaught and looked appealingly at Charles.

'It's all right,' he said, reaching across the table and patting her hand—an action which only served to increase Damon's anger, for his eyes now blazed white-hot as he pushed himself up from the table, rocking it so violently that the milk in the jug slopped over on to the cloth.

He raked his fingers through his hair. 'For heaven's sake Father, not you too?'

Charles stood up and faced the younger man. They were of equal height and looking at the two of them together it was easy to see what Damon would be like in another twenty-five years' time. Still handsome, still able to attract the girls—but that was not the reason Corrie was staying, and Charles knew it, even though his son seemed under a misapprehension.

'My son, you have it all wrong. Corrie is going to help me with my book. You know I've always said I needed a secretary—well, now I have one.'

Damon turned slowly and looked down at Corrie and the contempt on his face made her feel like crawling beneath the table, but instead she tilted her chin defiantly. 'Isn't it wonderful?' she said brightly. 'Now you won't have to worry about me and maybe I'll be able to save enough of my salary to get myself back home once your father's book is finished.'

Damon shook his head, as if unable to believe what he had heard. 'You're mad, Father, completely mad! Do you think I don't know what's going through your mind?'

'Call me an old fool if you like,' smiled Charles, undaunted, 'but I think I know what I'm doing. At least give me the benefit of the doubt. Only time will tell.'

Still shaking his head, Damon left the kitchen and Corrie breathed a sigh of relief. She was still perplexed. Their conversation had meant nothing to her, but she was glad he had gone. The tension had been so great it was like a time-bomb about to go off. One false move and there would have been an explosion.

'I'm sorry about that,' said Charles. He too looked relieved as he resumed his seat. 'Please don't let Damon worry you. I take people as I find them and so far as I'm concerned you're an extremely likeable young lady—and I'm going to enjoy working with you.'

'I'm glad, but do you think it wise?' A frown creased her normally smooth brow and she bit her lip anxiously. 'Damon might make things unpleasant for me and much as I'm

296-2691

looking forward to the work it might be as well if I went now, before I cause any more upsets in your household.'

'Nonsense, I can deal with Damon. As soon as we've finished breakfast you ring your family—they're the ones you should be concerned about. Do you think they'll raise any objections?'

They wouldn't be pleased, that much she knew, but there was nothing they could do about it. 'They're reasonable people,' she said, 'I think they'll understand.' John would be the one to object and she could not really blame him. She had not even bothered to send him a card, hoping that Anne and David would pass on the message that she had arrived safely.

Once their meal was over Corrie offered to wash up, but Charles insisted that she phone her parents, while he himself tidied the kitchen. 'I'm used to it,' he said. 'Damon spends most of his time putting the estate into order and organising the builders, so I run the house as well as trying to write my book. It will be a big help, having you here. You don't know how much I'm looking forward to it.'

Anne herself answered the telephone and squealed in surprise when she heard Corrie's voice. 'Darling, where are you? We've been wondering how you were getting on. Have you found—' her voice faltered, 'who you were looking for?'

'No,' said Corrie, and thought she detected a sigh of relief at the other end of the line. 'But, Mom, there's something else. I—I've got a job here.'

A long silence before Anne said, 'What sort of job?' and her voice sounded as though she was having great difficulty in controlling it.

'A kind of secretary, I suppose.' Corrie did not quite know how to put it.

'But where will you live?' asked Anne. 'Are you sure you know what you're doing?'

'It—it's a living-in job. I've met this man who's writing a book on the history of his house and he wants me to help him.'

'A man?' Anne sounded suspicious.

'Oh, there's nothing like that,' laughed Corrie. 'He's about sixty and rather a dear. Will you let Mr Higgins know I won't be coming back—and Mom, tell John I'll be writing.'

'He won't like this, you know.' A note of anger crept into Anne's voice. 'He was complaining he hadn't heard from you. You're not being fair on him, Corrie, I can't think what's got into you. Why don't you come home and let us discuss this thing rationally?'

'There's nothing to discuss,' insisted

58

Corrie. 'I know what I'm doing. Just tell him that, will you?' Her voice rose slightly and she was about to put down the receiver when Charles appeared at her elbow.

'Let me speak to her,' he whispered, and took the phone before she could refuse, gesturing that she return to the kitchen and leave him to deal with her mother.

The murmur of his voice reached her, but she could not hear what he said. When he came into the kitchen a minute or two later, though, he was smiling, satisfied. 'I think I've convinced her that you're in safe hands.'

'Thanks,' she said, relieved. 'Did she say anything about John?'

'Oh yes, she said quite a lot about your young man, so I told her that if he wants to satisfy himself about your well being to come on over. He'll be quite welcome.'

'Oh!' Corrie knew it would be ungrateful to say that she didn't want him here. But she didn't. The trouble was she was not sure why. It was as though John belonged to another world and was no part of this new chapter that had just begun. She loved him, of course she did, and she was going to marry him, but as for him being here—well, she would prefer him not to come. There was nothing she could do about it now, though, so she smiled, 'That will be nice, thank you.'

59

'So it's all settled.' Charles rubbed his hands together gleefully. 'Do you know, I oughtn't to say this, but I'm glad you had your car stolen. Otherwise Damon would never have brought you here and I wouldn't have had the good fortune of finding someone to help me with my book.'

It was impossible not to be affected by his enthusiasm. 'I'm glad it had its usefulness,' she replied lightly, 'but I hope it will be found. I shall need it when I get back home.'

He nodded. 'I'm sure it will be. Now, what shall we do next? Would you like to look over the house? I can show you my study and your room, you can have the one with the view— you'll like that, I know.'

He was sprightly for his age and as Corrie followed him out of the kitchen she could not help comparing him with his son. Their personalities were as different as chalk from cheese. Whereas Damon's was forceful and dominant, tempered by a ruthless aggression, his father's was mild and patient and she guessed he would never lose his temper or judge her unfairly.

But it was the son who held her mind captive. Despite his arrogant attitude she was aware of a growing attraction, not altogether due to his devastating good looks. No, it was more than that, he exuded a strong physical magnetism that she could not ignore. She need have no fear, however, that he would ever make any passes at her. He had made his feelings perfectly clear.

CHAPTER FOUR

'This is my study,' Charles' voice broke into Corrie's thoughts as they came to a halt at a door beneath the wide stairs. 'You'll have to excuse the mess, but I'm relying on you to put me in order.'

It was certainly chaos. Beneath the window was a huge desk with a typewriter practically covered beneath a mound of papers and maps. Bookshelves along two walls held a miscellany of books pushed in haphazardly; more books stood in piles on the floor. An easy chair occupied one corner with a small table beside it on which sat a plate with a curled-up sandwich and a cup of tea with a grey skin on top.

'I never got round to them,' Charles said apologetically. 'I get so engrossed sometimes I forget to eat.'

Corrie made a mental note to put a stop to that. He would have proper meals at regular hours even if she had to cook them herself, which looked as though it might be the case. She did not mind, in fact it would be a challenge to keep house for the two Courtneys. One of them at least would appreciate it—she was not so sure about the other.

Only one room downstairs was habitable, a large comfortable-looking sitting room with a superbly sculptured fireplace which dominated the room. Logs were heaped in readiness for lighting and Corrie could already imagine the warmth they would give. Again there was a red carpet with swirls of gold which were echoed in the long velvet curtains. A settee covered in brocade in a paler shade of gold with two matching armchairs occupied the central floor area, while against the walls were a drinks cupboard and a magnificent carved sideboard in mahogany. Two side tables completed the room, also exquisitely carved with foliage and birds.

It was an elegant room, yet not one that she would be afraid to use. 'It's beautiful,' she said to Charles, who had watched her scrutiny with smiling interest.

'I'm hoping to restore the other rooms up to this standard,' he said. 'All the furniture's there, shrouded of course, but it takes time and I think that the outside is of prime importance while the weather is fine. Let's go upstairs now.

'This is my room.' He opened a door next to the dressing room which she had used earlier and Corrie had a glimpse of an unmade bed and clothes slung across chairs. 'I'm not the tidiest of men,' he apologised. 'When I can't find anything then I have a good clean out.'

'I expect you miss your wife,' said Corrie sympathetically.

His face softened. 'I do, more than anyone knows.'

'If you like,' she said a shade hesitantly, 'I'll tidy it up for you, that is if you don't mind me going into your room?'

'Oh, no,' said Charles instantly. 'This is no part of your job. You mustn't feel obliged to do anything other than help me with my book.'

'But I'd like to,' she insisted gently. 'I don't mind housework, honestly I don't, and I love cooking, if I can be of any help in that direction.'

Charles looked down at her, his face working curiously. 'You're like an angel from heaven,' he said, 'and I'll be pleased to accept—sometimes—but not on a regular basis. If I find you doing too much I shall be angry.'

Corrie could not see this mild man getting cross with her, he in no way had the same hasty disposition as his son. She wondered whether Damon had inherited it from his mother and for the first time felt curious about the woman whose dress she wore. She would have dearly loved to ask questions, but decided it was too early yet in their relationship to expect Charles to confide intimate details such as this.

'This is the room I thought you might like.' Charles had opened another door opposite and Corrie gasped in pleasure. Gold again was very much in evidence, but this time coupled with blue. A rich cornflower-blue carpet patterned in a beige and gold traditional design, a monster of a bed with a gold silk cover, embroidered elaborately in blue with a bird of prey, a mahogany wardrobe and dresser carved with grotesque faces.

Charles said, 'Such carvings are the hallmark of Irish furniture. I trust you don't find them unpleasant?'

Corrie ran her finger over the monstrous carved faces, tracing the bulbous eyes and the wide snarling mouths. 'I think they're fun,' she said unexpectedly. It certainly added character to the room, if nothing else.

The tall window, magnificently curtained in blue brocade, was where she made her way next and the view quite took her breath away. The bedroom she had used last night had looked out on nothing more than tall fir trees, hiding completely whatever lay beyond, but here the view was uninterrupted and completely breathtaking.

Their climb yesterday had brought them to the head of a valley and from this vantage point Corrie could see along its entire length, from the misty distant mountains to the closer tree-clad slopes, the fields in varying shades of green, a glitter of water from a half-hidden lake. Larch and fir framed her view. It was spectacular and awe-inspiring and she knew she would never tire of looking from this particular spot, each time noticing something different.

On her first day in Ireland she had felt an affinity with the country, and now this feeling went deeper, bonding her inexorably to this small island and her people.

Her eyes were moist when she looked round at Charles, but she did not need to speak. He understood her sentiments completely and she guessed that it had had the same effect on him when he first came here. How lucky he was, she thought; what a marvellous inheritance. 'Tell me about Hawksmoor,' she said. 'How did it get its name?'

'We'll look outside while I tell you,' he answered, his hand solicitously beneath her elbow as he led her back down the wide stairs.

She discovered that the entrance they had used last night was at the back of the house. Now Charles took her through a massive oak door at the front. They stood for a few moments on the portico, looking across at the valley, before making their way down the stone steps which led to the gardens.

'This valley,' he said, 'is known as the Valley of the Hawk, hence Hawksmoor. So far as I've been able to gather the first owner of this house was interested in falconry. He bred hawks and used them for catching game. That was how the valley got its name, but it was a pity, for the wild life never came back in the same degree.'

'The reason for the hawk on my bedspread?' asked Corrie, lifting her delicately arched brows.

'That's right. I doubt if that was made all those years ago, but someone must have had it made somewhere along the line, and it seemed a pity not to use it.'

'I like it,' she said. 'It's like a personal emblem. Have you found any more references to the hawk?'

He nodded. 'On the gateposts are two stone hawks and in one of the rooms yet to be decorated are hawks carved into the fireplace, as well as a coat of arms at present away being restored.'

Looking back at the house Corrie was now able to see clearly its impressive size. There was a central block flanked on either side by wings set at an angle. The windows on the ground floor were pedimented and supported by consoles. It all looked very grand, if somewhat neglected, and she could well understand Charles' pride in his inheritance. She was really looking forward to learning about his family.

The gardens near to the house were formal with the lawns neatly trimmed and the rose beds dug, but further afield it looked as though the gardens melted into the valley itself. Shrubs grew with careless abandon, flowers struggled to push their pretty heads through a riot of weed and grasses—a careless wild splendour that added instead of detracted to the beauty of this isolated estate.

'We try to be self-sufficient,' explained Charles. 'We have cows and lambs, a few hens and some pigs—and over there is the vegetable garden. Damon has help, when they bother to turn up, but for the most part he does everything himself. He works hard, too hard I think, but it makes no difference what I say. He has some bee in his bonnet that we need help from no one. He won't even let me get a woman to help run the house.'

Corrie recalled Damon telling her that they

67

found it impossible to keep anyone. Why had he misled her? 'He hates women, doesn't he?' she questioned. 'Perhaps that's why.'

'It could be,' agreed Charles. 'I still can't get over him bringing you here.'

'I'm glad he did,' she admitted candidly. 'I wouldn't have fancied a night spent beneath a hedge.'

Charles laughed. 'You'd have had help from somewhere. No one in their right mind would let a pretty girl like you sleep rough.'

Back in the house Corrie volunteered to prepare the vegetables for lunch, as Charles had already told her that as it was Sunday he would not expect her to start work today.

At first he had objected, but soon gave in when she used her charming smile to get her own way. It usually worked and she had used it many times on John when he had wanted to do something and she didn't. Like going to football matches. He was mad keen about the game, but she herself could not stand it and had always flatly refused to go, generally being able to persuade him that he would much rather go to a movie or a walk in their local park.

It made her wonder whether it would work on Damon. Somehow she doubted it. His antagonism was so great it would take more than a smile to melt it. 'He's like a stone,' she said, talking to herself, for Charles had left her a few minutes earlier, murmuring something about making his bed, 'hard and impregnable. I wonder if anyone has ever got through to him?'

She had the tap full on, running water into the bowl ready for peeling the potatoes, and did not hear the door open and close and was unaware that Damon stood close behind her. 'Are you talking about me?' he asked.

She spun round wildly, her heart pumping at an alarming rate when she found herself confronted by those probing grey eyes. She had forgotten how cold they could look, but despite his disapproving stance it made no difference to the quagmire of emotions his nearness aroused.

She could not understand it and knew she must look foolish, her mouth wide open and her eyes apprehensive, but only for the few seconds it took her to gain control of herself. 'I was,' she said coldly.

'And would it surprise you to hear that the answer is no?' he continued. 'For your information, because you seem interested, I've never yet found a woman who has, what shall I say, penetrated the chink in my armour, and it's no good you trying with your beguiling little smile which works so well on my father, because it won't do any good.'

'You flatter yourself if you think I'm interested,' she returned scornfully, while at the same time fully realising that the very fact he had heard her speaking her thoughts aloud revealed that he had been on her mind.

'Then it must be my father,' he said, 'and he's just as bad if he's been taken in by your pretty face. It's true, the saying that there's no fool like an old fool, but I wouldn't have thought a man of his age would appeal to you. What's happened—fed up with chasing the boys?'

'You're despicable!' she spat, turning back to the sink and plunging her hands into the bowl of water. 'I'm working for your father, full stop. If you think anything else then you're perverted!'

'If you knew what I know you might not think that accusation so improbable,' he said, 'but what I want to know right now is what you're doing in that dress? It's far too old for you, don't you know that?'

'Considering it was your mother's it's not surprising.' She picked up a potato and attacked it with the knife. 'But after you'd pushed me into that deplorable room and I'd slept all night in my dress what did you expect me to do? Take it off and wash it and run around in my undies? Oh, damn!' The point of the knife jagged into her thumb and she

70

spun about, sucking the wounded finger. 'Well, did you?'

But he ignored her last question, saying instead, in a tight-lipped voice, 'That dress was not my mother's.'

She looked down at the blue material, horrified to notice the spot of blood staining the front. 'Perhaps you never saw her in it, but I can assure you it's hers. Charles told me to help myself from her wardrobe.'

Damon's eyes narrowed at her use of his father's Christian name. 'Then he must have conveniently forgotten to tell you that she's my *step*mother. God help me if she'd been my real mother,' he added bitterly. 'I hate her. Shall I tell you what she is—or would it be sufficient to say that she sleeps around with anyone who'll have her? Father knew it, but he was so besotted by her beautiful face and fabulous figure that he forgave her anything. Anything, do you hear? Poor misguided fool!'

Corrie felt the colour drain from her cheeks. Poor Charles—but if he had been happy what right had Damon to criticise? 'I don't see that it's any business of yours what type of a person she is, if your father's in love with her that's all that matters.'

'Oh, he was that all right—when she was here.' Anguished lines creased Damon's face and his eyes flamed until Corrie felt a real

71

physical fear. 'Shall I tell you the name of this—harlot?' His hands shot out and gripped her shoulders, so that there was no escape even had she wanted to.

'Zelah Cunningham—now Zelah Courtney!' He spat out the name, his hands tightening when Corrie struggled to escape.

'I don't believe you,' she cried, 'you're lying! You're only saying this to hurt me.' But even while she denied it, deep down inside she knew it was true. Right from the first day when that scruffy boy had told her Zelah had kissed him she had known something was wrong, that the woman was not all she had thought. But not this—not anything so awful as this! She covered her face with her hands, swallowing hard, trying desperately to stem the tears that had already moistened her eyes.

Realising that he had perhaps hurt her enough, Damon let her go, standing back, his arms folded, watching her critically. 'The news has shaken you, I see. Have I shatterd your illusions? A pity, but then life is like that, full of hard knocks.'

'You needn't have delivered it quite so offensively.'

'Why should I be tactful?' he queried. 'It's the truth. A pity there's no divorce in Ireland. She clings like a vine, coming back when the mood takes her, though this time I must admit it's been a long time—six months, no less. Perhaps she's met someone else, some other rich man who's taken her fancy.'

Corrie was still recovering from the shock and her voice wavered despite an attempt to appear in control. 'He must have entered into marriage with his eyes open.'

'Infatuation, flattery, call it what you like, but it certainly wasn't love he felt for her, and I doubt if she loved him. That woman is incapable of loving anyone except herself— and money, of course.' He paused before saying quite deliberately. 'Why are you looking for her?'

But Corrie was in no mood at this moment to tell him. His revelation had shattered her and she wanted nothing more than to be alone. 'Mind your own business!' she cried, racing from the kitchen to her room, where she slammed the door and flung herself on to the bed.

It hurt—this thought that her mother was of easy virtue. Yet it must have started nineteen years ago when she herself was born. That had been the beginning. How many more unwanted children had she conceived, or had she been frightened by that first mistake and taken precautions ever since? Corrie hoped so. She would not want anyone else to feel as miserable as she did now.

73

The dress she wore felt suddenly tainted, and not purely by the bloodstain. With trembling fingers she tore it off, discarding it in a crumpled heap on the floor, looking down at it distastefully. With a vicious movement she kicked the offending garment. It flew through the air and the door opened at the same time so that the folds of the material hit Charles Courtney squarely in the face.

'Oh, I'm sorry,' she cried hastily. 'I didn't mean to—I had no idea that—oh, dear, what must you think?'

'Never mind that now,' he said, shaking his head. 'Have you argued with Damon? I heard your raised voices and you scuttling along the landing. What's the matter, child? You look as white as a ghost.'

Corrie stared at Charles, her lips trembling and her large eyes like blue shadows, forgetting that she wore nothing but her bra and pants.

'Sit down,' he said kindly, 'before you fall down, and here, wrap this round you,' pulling the blue cover from the bed and holding it out like a cape.

She accepted gracefully and sank down on to the edge of the bed, relieved to get the weight off her trembling limbs. The problem now was what to tell Charles Courtney. It couldn't be anything less than the truth, for his son would be certain to relate the facts when they next met.

But how to begin, and how to put it in such a manner that she did not hurt him? If, as Damon had said, it was true and he still did think a lot of Zelah, she would not like to say anything detrimental about her. The trouble was there was not one nice thing she could say. The whole affair left a bitter taste in her mouth and she wished she had never insisted on trying to find her mother.

'I think I know,' he said, when after a few minutes it became clear that she was not going to speak. 'He objected to you wearing that dress?'

Corrie nodded, glad he had guessed; it should make her task easier. 'He told me who it belonged to. I had no idea you'd married a second time—I'm sorry she's left you.'

He grimaced but did not appear unduly perturbed. There was a chair near the door and he pulled it up so that he sat opposite, holding her one free hand as with the other she held the silk cover closely about her.

'I've got used to her comings and goings, but despite what my son might have told you I still love her, in my own way. She's very beautiful and I like beautiful things about me, as you've probably noticed. So I can afford to ignore her—indiscretions. When she's here she's all I could ask for in a wife. At my age what more can I desire? I'm flattered that she should find me attractive.'

Corrie felt sad and squeezed the big hand holding her own. 'Bless you, Charles, for thinking like that. I guess she doesn't deserve it, but I'm glad if she gives you some measure of happiness.' She paused, choosing her next words carefully. 'There's something I think you should know—the real reason I came to Ireland.'

'It's connected with Zelah?'

His blue eyes held her own and she saw there not pain, but hope, and for a moment she was at a loss to understand. 'That's right,' she said. 'I only discovered a week ago that she was—she is—'

'Your mother?' Charles finished for her. 'Anne told me you were looking for her and from the first moment I saw you I knew you had to be related. You're so like her, my dear, so very much like her.' He smiled. 'Except that you have a naïveté about you that Zelah never had. Don't ever lose your innocence, child.'

He pulled her to him and Corrie had the feeling that he was as close to tears as she was herself. 'That wasn't why you offered me the job?' she asked shakily, surprised that he had discussed so much with Anne in the few

76

minutes he had been on the phone.

'No, no, of course not. That had nothing to do with it—well, at least not much,' he added honestly. 'Oh, Corrie, do you know what this means to me? You're the daughter I always wanted and never had. I'm so happy.' And this time tears did slide down his cheeks and Corrie wiped them away with a finger before lifting her face to bestow an affectionate kiss on his damp cheek.

It was not until he had pushed her gently away that a shock wave ran through her. If Charles was her stepfather, that meant that Damon was—her stepbrother! A more daunting situation would be difficult to find.

'What we must do now,' said Charles brightly, 'is find you something to wear. There are a couple of dresses in Zelah's wardrobe that she's never worn. Take your pick of those and then tomorrow Damon can run you into Wicklow. Zelah has an account in one of the shops there; get what you need.'

'I couldn't!' cried Corrie, aghast at the idea of him spending so much money on her. A whole new wardrobe of clothes was not cheap.

'Nonsense,' returned Charles. 'You have no choice.'

He was right, of course. 'Well, only if you'll let me pay you back when I have some money transferred.'

77

Charles shrugged. 'Very well, call it a loan, but there's no rush. You might need that money sometime, don't rob yourself on my behalf.'

Corrie did not like the idea, still less was she looking forward to the thought of Damon taking her, but without transport of her own there was no alternative. She hoped it would not be long before her own car was found; she must remember to ask Damon whether he had contacted the police.

The dress she chose was in grass-green cotton with a close-fitting bodice and a billowing skirt. It accentuated her tiny waist and the scooped neckline revealed her creamy skin.

Even though she knew that Zelah had never worn this garment it was constantly in her mind that it had been bought by her, and Corrie knew she would not feel satisfied until she had some clothes of her own.

She wondered whether to ask Anne to send some over, and then thought of the expense and the trouble, and the explanations it would incur when she had to tell them her car had been stolen. Anne would worry even more than she must now; it would be wise to say nothing and manage as best she could on the few clothes she would purchase tomorrow.

Back in the kitchen Charles had taken over

preparing their lunch, but Corrie insisted on helping and decided to bake an apple pie. 'You'll spoil us,' laughed Charles. 'We've had no home baking since my first wife—er—well, for a long time.'

'Then it's time you did,' she said severely, appreciating his reluctance to talk about the first Mrs Courtney. She donned a huge butcher-type apron that she found hanging behind the door. 'Tell me where everything's kept and I'll have it done in no time.'

There was a happy-go-lucky atmosphere in the kitchen until Damon came in shortly before lunch. Then Corrie stopped talking, carrying on with the custard she was making, but very much aware of the tension his presence caused. He washed his hands at the sink, told his father that one of the cows was sick and he was going to call in the vet, and then disappeared again.

Between them Corrie and Charles laid the table and served the meal, Damon appearing as if on cue when everything was ready. He had changed out of his working jeans into a pair of thigh-hugging black trousers topped by a thin roll-necked sweater, also in black. He looked satanical, yet devilishly attractive, thought Corrie, trying to ignore the now almost familiar racing of her heart his presence caused. His thick dark hair, still damp from the shower, curled into his nape, his eyes were alive and watchful, waiting until she was seated before sitting down himself.

They ate in silence for a few minutes before Charles said, 'Damon, will you take Corrie into Wicklow tomorrow? She needs some new clothes—you know where to go?'

Damon nodded, his eyes critical as they returned to Corrie. 'Let's hope you're not so extravagant as my stepmother. Poor Father had a shock every time he received their account.'

'It was not my idea,' snapped Corrie, 'and for your information, I'm only having a loan. I intend to pay back every penny. I want no favours from you Courtneys, nor do I expect any.'

'Corrie,' said Charles quietly, 'take no notice of my son. He's very rude, even though I suspect he's only teasing. He can be very cruel without realising it.'

'Can I, Father?' asked Damon. 'You misunderstand me. I meant every word I said, I don't like to see you fleeced.'

'I'm sure Corrie would never do that,' Charles reproved.

The younger man's eyes narrowed as much as to say, 'We'll see,' but for the remainder of the meal he veered off the subject, discussing instead the progress of the work on the outside

80

of the house.

Corrie noticed he ate his apple pie with relish, but he made no comment, leaving the room immediately he had finished.

She was relieved when he had gone because his presence dominated the tiny kitchen, there being a vitality about him she found impossible to ignore. Indeed he was a man no one could ever fail to notice. It was a pity he had this thing about women, for she was sure he would make a fantastic lover. Her cheeks flamed at this sudden unbidden thought and she bent her head, collecting the empty plates and loading them into the dishwasher so that Charles should not see and perhaps ask embarrassing questions.

The rest of the day passed uneventfully. Corrie did not see Damon again and his father made no mention of him, so clearly he knew where he was. She was afraid to ask for fear of arousing Charles' curiosity as to why she wanted to know.

She slept well in the big blue bed but woke feeling definitely apprehensive. Today she was going into Wicklow with Damon, today she would be at the mercy of his biting tongue.

Charles had told her to use Zelah's dressing room and as she slipped across the landing clutching a diaphanous negligee about her, she looked anxiously at the door next to hers hoping that Damon would not appear. His father had indicated yesterday which was his room, but he had not volunteered to show her inside and she guessed that this was Damon's private sanctum, with no one allowed in unless by invitation.

Hurriedly she washed and slipped once again into the green dress, brushing her hair until it shone like spun silk. She was looking forward to buying some make-up as she felt bare without it, but nothing would induce her to touch the endless bottles and tubes that Zelah had left behind.

After Damon's revelation about her true character Corrie felt a cold shiver pass over her every time she thought about this woman. It was a cruel quirk of fate that had made this despicable person her mother, and she knew that for as long as she lived she would never think of her again in this capacity.

At least it made her appreciate Anne and David all the more, and she knew that Anne's relief would be boundless when she returned home. She wondered whether Anne had known all along about the sort of life her friend's sister had led, whether this had been the real reason behind her trying to dissuade her from setting out on this search. At least Anne need have no further qualms about the future, she need never fear that Corrie would leave her again. When she returned to marry John everything would be as it was before, this whole episode would be forgotten.

Or would it? And did she still want to marry John?

For the first time doubts crept into her mind and she could not help comparing John with Damon. The difference between the two men was marked. John was good and kind, possessing average good looks; indeed he was the average kind of man, and she had no doubt that he loved her and would make a good husband.

Damon on the other hand was a tall handsome devil, the sort every woman would turn her head to take a second look. Not that it would do her any good. His hatred of the opposite sex had turned him into a hard, bitter man; his eyes, eyes that were well shaped and framed by thick dark lashes, were always cold and could pierce through a person as though they were made of steel. His lips were ruthless and she herself had felt the whip of his tongue. But in spite of all this there was a certain something about him that attracted her, a magnetism that impelled her towards him. His virility could not be ignored.

This trip into Wicklow today could prove a dangerous mission. It all depended on

Damon's attitude. If he was as rude as he had been yesterday lunchtime, it did not augur well for the time they must inevitably spend together.

As she made her way downstairs Corrie could not quell the uneven beating of her heart. It was only by sheer determination that she was able to keep a smile on her lips when she entered the kitchen and came face to face with Damon's cold, almost insolent greeting.

'Be prepared, Miss Maitland. Don't overspend. I shall be watching you like a hawk.'

CHAPTER FIVE

Damon's greeting infuriated Corrie, but she kept her anger hidden and smiled politely. 'That won't be necessary. I only intend buying the bare necessities.' She sat down on a kitchen chair opposite him. 'Despite what you might think, it was your father who insisted.'

'Why would that be,' he asked, 'when he'd already told you to make use of Zelah's clothes?'

Reluctant to admit that he had been the reason, she shook her head haughtily. 'Let's say I had second thoughts about wearing thcm.'

'Or you told him what I said,' goaded Damon, 'and dear Father, poor fool that he is, offered to buy you some new ones. You could have turned him down,' he added angrily.

'I could have,' she snapped, 'but Charles would have been hurt.' She popped some bread into the toaster and poured herself a cup of tea.

'That's rich,' he sneered. 'Since when would a woman of your type be concerned whether she hurt anyone?'

Corrie clenched her teeth. To argue with Damon now would make their forthcoming trip impossible. He was an arrogant, sarcastic beast at the best of times, but to be at loggerheads with him for the whole time they were out was more than she felt up to. 'I'm sorry your opinion of me is so low, Mr Courtney. Be assured I'll do my best not to offend even your sense of outrage.' She spread butter and marmalade on to her toast and bit into it, as the same time looking at him with her large wistful eyes. 'You could try giving me the benefit of the doubt.'

'Unless proved otherwise,' he countered drily. 'I might do just that, Miss Maitland, and as you're calling my father Charles it might be as well if you called me Damon.'

Corrie shrugged lightly. 'As you wish.' He

85

was already Damon in her thoughts, anyway. She continued to finish her toast and drink her tea, vitally aware of his regard. It was as though for some reason he was trying to assess her, to find out whether she was cast in the same mould as he seemed to think all women were. 'Let me know your conclusions,' she said flippantly.

He frowned, not immediately aware of the line her thoughts had taken.

'You were studying me intently,' she explained with a brief smile, 'so I feel entitled to know exactly what's going through your mind.'

He laughed. 'You wouldn't believe me if I told you.' He scraped back his chair. 'I'll go and start the car. Meet me outside.'

Knowing that it would be inadvisable to keep him waiting, Corrie hurried the remainder of her breakfast. She was glad it was another warm sunny day as it removed the necessity of wearing one of Zelah's coats.

The Rolls was ticking over, purring as smoothly as a kitten. Corrie climbed into its plush interior, sinking into the depths of the seat and sniffing appreciatively the leather upholstery. Here was luxury!

Damon scarcely glanced at her, easing the car forward along the curved rhododendron-lined drive. His close proximity caused a wild fluttering within her breast and she was glad that he could not see her agitation. It would be the height of humiliation for him to discover the effect he had on her, for it would probably confirm his suspicions that she was conforming to the pattern in which he classed all her sex.

It was equally puzzling to her why he should have this effect. The way he treated her certainly did not warrant such feelings— all she knew was that the man's overwhelming personality did it—forceful, as explosive as dynamite, but with a powerful masculinity that turned her on and made her limbs feel as though they were made of jelly.

She stole a glance at his profile, the hawklike nose and the broad forehead above which sprang thick black hair, as unruly as the man himself. She felt an urge to run her fingers through it, to feel for herself its wiry strength, to trace the harsh lines of his jaw and touch those full mobile lips which were at this moment set into a straight line.

He clearly resented having to take her into Wicklow this morning, and she could understand it. No doubt he had work to do that was more important than buying clothes for the girl he had begrudgingly brought back to his house when she had idiotically lost all her belongings.

She licked her lips anxiously. 'I'm sorry to put you to all this trouble.' Her voice was scarcely more than a whisper and when he did not answer, when his expression did not alter, she thought he had not heard. Clearing her throat, she said in a louder voice, 'Damon, I really am sorry. If you like, we can go back. I—I'll manage without new clothes.'

'Don't be a martyr,' he said harshly, glancing at her for one brief second. There was no softening in those flint-like eyes and for the first time she noticed the darker line round the edge of the grey. They were beautiful eyes and she wondered what it would be like to have them looking at her with admiration instead of this cold scrutiny to which she was always subjected.

'I was only thinking of you—and your work,' she said in a hurt little voice. 'How about the sick cow, won't she need your attention?'

'She'll be all right for a few hours. It was milk fever.'

'What's that?' she asked, noticing how the tone of his voice had changed when he spoke of the animal. He thought more of the cow than her and she didn't know whether to find it funny or annoying.

'Without going into technicalities,' he said obligingly, 'the cow calved a day or so ago, but she went suddenly off her feed and started to blow up. The vet injected her and she's all right now, but I'll still have to keep my eye on her for a day or two.'

'Can I see the calf?' asked Corrie. It was all new to her, this farming business. Having lived in a town all her life, and not having had even a dog or cat because Anne was allergic to them, she had never had anything to do with animals.

'Sure,' he replied, surprisingly, 'so long as you don't get in my way. You might even be able to give me a hand, I could do with one sometimes.'

This was the nearest he had come to accepting her and Corrie would have loved to agree to help, but her loyalties lay with Charles. 'I'm sorry,' she said, 'I have work to do,' adding eagerly, 'in my spare time, though, I'd love to help.'

The brief glimpse she had seen of a warm human being had disappeared. 'Oh, my father—I'd forgotten,' he said coldly. 'Perhaps it's as well, you'd probably be a hindrance.'

When Corrie opened her mouth to protest he forestalled her by saying, 'Don't forget I've had an insight into your stupidity. I couldn't afford such expensive mistakes with the animals.'

'Everyone's allowed one mistake,' retaliated Corrie hotly. 'Are you going to persist in holding it against me?'

'Until I have reason to believe otherwise. So far the only good thing about you is that you can cook. Zelah was hopeless at anything domesticated, so that at least is one thing you haven't got in common.'

Corrie remained silent, wondering whether Damon had learned from his father the relationship between them. She felt sure he hadn't, for if he knew he would undoubtedly taunt her with it. He seemed to take a great delight in making her feel uncomfortable.

'What's the matter?' he asked, after the silence had lengthened between them. 'Don't you like me mentioning Zelah? Have you given up the idea of trying to find her or has my father temporarily distracted you from your search?'

And he did not mean by the writing, that much she knew. He had some bee in his bonnet that she had made a play for Charles Courtney and the idea sickened her.

'You're disgusting!' she flared. 'How could you even think such a thing? He's old enough to be my grandfather!'

'Exactly.' Damon's tones were brutal, whipping her by their intensity. 'So why don't you let me take you back to England and forget this silly game you're playing?'

'Game!' echoed Corrie. 'You don't know what you're talking about. Charles and I understand each other, which is more than I can say for you. You have it in your mind that I'm as bad as my mo—as Zelah,' she finished hastily, cursing herself for the slip and hoping that Damon had not noticed.

Unfortunately he had. 'What were you going to say before you corrected yourself?' His brows beetled together in a frown.

He knew! He must know! He was just taking a wicked delight in extracting the information from her. 'Why should I tell you? It's none of your business.'

'Oh, but it is.' For one moment his attention was diverted as he negotiated a particularly nasty double bend. 'I think there's something you should tell me, young lady, something that matters very much to us both.'

Corrie shrugged. What did it matter? If he hadn't already guessed Charles would tell him sooner or later. 'Zelah is my mother,' she said bluntly, afraid now to look at his face, staring instead straight ahead at the ribbon of road curving away out of sight.

Damon let out a long low whistle and brought the car to a halt. 'So that's it! I thought maybe you were sisters, that's why

I—but mother and daughter—I can't believe it. She must have been still a schoolgirl when she had you!'

'Sixteen—and I'm illegitimate,' she added defiantly, 'in case you were wondering.'

'It makes sense,' he said savagely. 'I wonder how many more brats she's brought into the world—unwanted, unloved.'

Corrie shivered under the intensity of his anger. It was a thought that had occurred to her, but for some inexplicable reason she felt obliged to stick up for the absent woman. 'It takes two to make a child,' she snapped, 'and with the world full of men ready to take advantage what do you expect?'

'When a woman flaunts herself like Zelah does, no man will refuse. Why should he?'

'And so you put the whole female sex into the same class? Maybe my mother is—easy game,' she conceded reluctantly, 'but that doesn't make me the same, or anyone else.'

'It does in my mind,' he stated categorically. 'I've never yet met anyone who hasn't been willing to fall into bed with me at the first meeting.'

It wasn't surprising, thought Corrie, with his shattering good looks and potent virile masculinity. It even caused her heart to flutter, and she hated him! 'Then you've been mixing with the wrong type,' she asserted flatly, staring out of the side window and refusing to look at him.

She was unprepared therefore when his fingers slid beneath her chin twisting her face towards him. 'Are you suggesting that you're different?' he rapped out. 'Do you really expect me to believe that my little bastard stepsister is any different from her mother?'

Corrie recoiled at the venom in his tone, grimacing beneath the painful pressure of his fingers. Her face blanched as she stared into the icy depths of his eyes, eyes that were censuring her as surely as if she herself had committed a crime. But from somewhere she found the strength to cry, 'How dare you! How dare you insult me when you know nothing at all about me!'

'I don't need to,' he said, 'one look at your tarty dyed hair is enough.'

So he had disbelieved her when she had told him it was natural. It did not seem worth arguing any more. She said dispiritedly, lifting her shoulders in a gesture of acceptance, 'I can see you've made up your mind as to the type of person I am. Perhaps time alone will make you change your opinion.'

'You won't be here that long,' he retorted quickly and heatedly. 'I shall make it my duty to see to that. I intend having a good long talk to Father. He's an old fool where women are concerned, but this time I intend to make sure he doesn't hurt himself again.'

Corrie compressed her lips stubbornly. Much more of this and she would be unable to control herself. Damon was possessed with the idea that she was after only one thing and to persistently deny it would get her nowhere. Silence was her best bet, silence and letting him think that he was right.

'What's the matter?' he sneered, 'have you nothing more to say for yourself? You know I'm right and have decided that arguing is pointless?' His face veered closer, accusing, hateful. 'Poor little Corrie, got yourself into deeper water than you expected?'

His taunting voice goaded Corrie into lashing out with all her strength, but as before he anticipated her action and releasing her chin caught her wrist, holding it against his chest. He hooked his other hand about her neck and pulled her towards him, his eyes blazing with an unfathomable emotion.

When he kissed her she was as shocked as if he had struck her and for a few long seconds remained frozen beneath his touch. But gradually, as the first numbness wore off, she became aware of the whole host of new emotions his embrace had triggered. She felt like a rose coming into full bloom. From a

94

tightly curled bud her feelings unfurled, slowly, deliciously, each movement sending quivers of delight along her nerves, until finally the whole gamut of her emotions were released.

Damon's kiss was like nothing else she had ever experienced. It was like a whirlwind inside her. John had never done this to her— his caress had left her warmly satisfied, yes, but never with this wanton craving for more, or this urge to feel his body close to hers, to be possessed by this man whom she professed to hate.

Her cheeks flamed at the line her thoughts were taking and she struggled to free herself. At the same time Damon thrust her from him, his face mirroring disgust. 'You're no better than she is,' he snapped cruelly. 'You're any man's for the taking, and don't bother to deny it, because it just won't work. I have the proof I need.'

Corrie sank back into her seat, confused and miserable. Was she like Zelah? Could it be that Damon was speaking the truth? She pressed her fingertips to her temples, her mind wildly searching for an answer.

If she was as wanton as he made out wouldn't she respond like this to John as well, or to any man who had kissed her in the past? Of course she would. It was just that Damon

95

was different, his physical magnetism would turn any woman on—he had said that himself.

She wished now that she had had the strength to resist him, the willpower to stop herself from responding to those kisses which had been surprisingly tender. She had expected his lovemaking to be as savage as his nature—unless he had done it deliberately, knowing full well the power he had. That was most likely the answer. He knew he had the ability to arouse a woman, no matter who, and he had used this weapon to prove the point he had been trying to make.

Her blue eyes flashed as she stared mutinously in his direction. He was preparing to start the engine, a satisfied smile curving his lips. 'You think you're so clever, *Mr* Courtney—what I wouldn't do to take you down a peg or two!'

'I hardly think you'll be able to do that,' he said pleasantly. 'It would take more than a slip of a girl to outwit me. Shall we continue our journey, we're wasting valuable time?'

Corrie swung away impatiently. 'Oh, go to hell!'

'Not a pleasant place,' he murmured, 'but some of us end up there, so I believe.'

Meaning that he thought she would, and Zelah, and anyone else he cared to throw into the same category. 'Perhaps you would know that better than I,' she said sweetly, determined to ignore him for the rest of their journey.

But this proved to be impossible, for it was as though, now he had convinced himself as to her type, he was prepared to be civil to her if nothing more, and he went on to explain the passing scenery. 'Most cottages in Ireland have turf fires,' he informed her, 'giving out a sweet scent that's quite unforgettable.'

Damon, waxing sentimental! She couldn't believe it.

'These piles,' he said, indicating turves stacked neatly at the edge of a bog, 'have different names according to their size. That's a turnfoot, and then there are castles and clamps, and rickles and reeks.'

'How do they cut them?' asked Corrie, interested despite herself. 'Isn't it dangerous? I mean, mightn't they sink?'

'They do it in April or May,' he said, 'the driest months, and those ridges are where they've spread the parings to walk on and wheel their barrows along while they dig out the turf.'

He went on to explain about the different methods of cutting, but it was all too complicated for Corrie to understand. She appreciated, though, him taking the time to tell her. 'What method has been used here?'

she asked, looking along the dark parallel trenches.

'Underfooting,' he explained. 'Soon the whole area will be waving with bog cotton and in the autumn it will change to russet and fiery red. Bogs can be very beautiful places, especially seen at dawn or dusk when the long rays of the sun give the earth a silken sheen.'

This was a side to Damon's nature Corrie had not seen and she was amazed. He had proved that he was not all mercenary, that there were moments when he could be as friendly as his fellow beings.

Their drive to Wicklow took them through some very beautiful countryside, but Damon did not stop again and Corrie wondered whether he regretted his momentary lapse.

Wicklow itself was a charming old-world town with narrow streets, but the store to which he took her looked expensive and Corrie began to have second thoughts about accepting Charles' loan. How would she ever afford to pay it back? She would need to be careful about what she bought—the very minimum to get her through until she had some money of her own, and then she could shop around at her discretion for something cheaper.

Damon was apparently a well-known figure here and was treated with a sort of revered respect. They were shown into the dress department and he sat down on a French gilt chair, one foot resting on his knee, an elbow across the back of the chair, his hand supporting his head which was turned critically towards her. Corrie knew that he meant what he had said earlier, but he need not worry. She herself would make sure that she did not spend too much.

When he insisted that she parade before him in each of the dresses in turn she felt like telling him to mind his own business—she was the one who had to wear the dresses, not he. But good manners, and the fact that the salesgirl found nothing strange in his request, suggesting that he had done this sort of thing before, made her succumb meekly to his wishes.

After she had tried on at least a dozen dresses, each one a delight to wear and making Corrie feel dizzy with the sheer pleasure of feeling these beautiful clothes next to her skin, Damon said, 'We'll take the white and the blue, that pinky thing and the one with the stripes.'

Corrie opened her mouth to protest and then closed it again. What did it matter? They were all equally desirable. It was just annoying to think that he felt he had the right to choose for her.

In the lingerie department she was relieved to find that he let her do her own choosing, and the same with shoes and cosmetics, but when she said she had now sufficient for her needs he said, 'How about casual wear, beach clothes and the like? Surely my father's not going to work you all day and every day? You will have some time to yourself?'

'I suppose so,' she admitted, 'but we haven't really discussed hours.'

They came out of the store with far more than Corrie had intended and she was surprised that Damon had allowed it. In the car, looking at the parcels piled on the back seat, she said, 'There looks an awful lot there. I'm sure I shan't wear half of them.'

'Then you're not like your mother,' he said, looking at her strangely. 'She would think nothing of buying herself half a dozen evening dresses or a dozen pairs of shoes.'

Compared to that, thought Corrie, she supposed her own purchases were meagre. It was no wonder Damon had warned her to be careful, if he thought she was of the same nature as Zelah.

Corrie had thought that after their shopping expedition he would drive straight back home and was surprised and pleased when he suggested they visit a place called Powerscourt. 'It has one of the finest

100

landscaped gardens in Ireland,' he explained. 'It's my ambition to have Hawksmoor looking equally grand one day.'

It was magnificent, there was no doubt about it. They stood in front of the splendidly timbered house, the ground falling away before them in a series of terraces. In the distance, beyond a wooded valley, rose the Wicklow Mountains, crowned by the smooth indigo of the Sugar Loaf.

They walked along the first terrace, down a broad flight of steps which led on to a wide lawn, and beyond was the focus of the whole garden—very wide, spiralling steps laid out in geometrical designs in black and white pebbles. There was a balustrade of intricate wrought iron and a pedestal with entwined bronze figures.

'Isn't it impressive?' asked Damon. 'Of course, this has been here for over a hundred years, but I have my plans. Hawksmoor will be a place of beauty too, when I've finished with it.'

There was a proud tilt to his head as he spoke and Corrie knew that he meant every word. It would be hard work, she knew, and in that moment, when they were as close together as they had ever been, she wished that she could help him create this dream. Of course it would be impossible. She would not be here that long. It would take years and years of hard work to restore Hawksmoor to its former glory. She felt saddened at the thought that she might never see the culmination of these plans.

'I'm sure you'll make a very good job of it,' she said.

He smiled and she was amazed at the difference it made. The harsh shadows smoothed out miraculously and his eyes, although still not accepting her, had lost some of their hardness. It was almost possible to believe that they might be friends, which was a laugh. They would never be that. Damon's animosity towards Zelah was now extended to her. He clearly thought that traits, good or bad, ran in families.

Perhaps, eventually, she would be able to show him that she was different. The trouble was, would there be time? He had said he was determined to oust her out, and she knew without being told that Damon was not a man to let anything stand in his way. Her only hope lay in his father. With Charles on her side maybe she stood a chance. Only time would tell.

They had walked down a further series of terraces and now stood before a pool. 'Triton's Pool,' said Damon, 'once called Juggy's Pond. I prefer its present name, don't you?'

Corrie nodded, gazing with admiration across the sheet of water which reflected the spruce and fir which grew about its banks. There was a statue of Pegasus, footpaths disappearing through the trees. It was all so perfect she could only stand and stare.

'It gets you, doesn't it?' said Damon, observing her almost hypnotic stance. 'Of course the Irish climate, mild in winter and moist in summer, encourages growth and we're able to grow the more exotic plants which would never survive in England. In these gardens alone are rare dragon trees and the blue gum, a cousin of the magnolia.'

'It's beautiful,' murmured Corrie.

'There's more to come, but we mustn't linger too long. I have work waiting to be done.'

She wished he hadn't said that. It made her feel guilty and she hurried along at his side, some of her pleasure gone out of the day. But her spirits soon revived when they walked along what Damon called Monkey Puzzle Avenue. On either side grew magnificent symmetrical dome-shaped monkey puzzles, tall and splendid, richly green. She had never seen anything quite like it.

And then, in contrast to the formality of these great gardens, he took her to see the waterfall. With immense force the water slid over the brow of a precipice, falling hundreds of feet in a glistening snowy white sheet, crashing into a dark pool and throwing up clouds of smoking spray. 'The force of it could knock out a man,' said Damon, 'and sometimes the wind reaches such a pitch here it's difficult to stand.'

Corrie was even more impressed. The effect of this natural phenomenon quite took her breath away and she looked up at Damon in wonder, minute particles of spray sparkling on her lips and brows, her blue eyes alight. He caught and held her gaze for a few heart-stopping seconds before saying tersely, 'It's time we went,' and led the way, striding ahead with his long legs, not even waiting to see whether she followed.

Corrie would have loved to know what had been in his mind at that precise moment, whether the waterfall had had the same effect on him as it had on herself. In some strange way it had excited her, bringing about a sexual awareness of the man at her side. She had wanted to reach out and take his hand so that together they might admire this great wonder.

She was convinced that he too had felt something, and that that was the reason why he had insisted they leave. She stared after his retreating back, more than a little aware that her feelings for him were growing by the hour.

CHAPTER SIX

Corrie was glad when they arrived back at Hawksmoor. The return journey had been uncomfortable to say the least. Damon had lapsed into his earlier aggressive mood, assuring her again that he intended to do all in his power to persuade his father against employing her.

Deciding that silence in this case would be prudent Corrie had said nothing; arguing would make him even more adamant and she was trying, if anything, to create a good impression.

However, his talk with Charles had to be postponed, for on their return he was called away to yet another emergency in the cowshed, not even staying to eat the lunch his father had cooked in their absence.

'How did it go?' asked Charles when they were settled at the table. 'Did you get everything?'

'Yes, thanks,' nodded Corrie, but she did not look as happy as Charles thought she should.

He said, 'Is Damon still against you working for me?'

He was shrewder than she thought. There

was not much that happened in this household of which he was not aware. 'He's going to have a word with you.' The words were out before she could stop them. 'Don't let him persuade you to send me away. I'm looking forward to this job so much.'

A warm smile creased Charles' face and his blue eyes softened. 'So am I, child, so am I.'

She knew then that he would fight his son, but the outcome would depend upon who was the stronger. Damon himself was determined and could be utterly ruthless when he desired. Charles on the other hand always appeared to her to be a kind, soft-hearted character. Perhaps he had hidden depths about which she knew nothing. She hoped so, she really did.

She tried to tell herself that the job was the sole reason for her wanting to stay here, something different from the normal run-of-the-mill routine to which she had been accustomed. That Damon was the attraction she refused to admit, though the niggling thought persistently crept into the back of her mind no matter how often she tried to push it away.

It was early evening before she saw Damon again. She had spent the afternoon putting away her purchases and helping Charles with the housework. He agreed that it was never-ending. With all the building work that was going on there was a perpetual film of dust over the whole house. A concrete mixer could be heard whirring away outside and the whistling of the workmen as they did their jobs.

When Damon came into the kitchen Corrie was putting the finishing touches to their meal. 'Where's my father?' he asked abruptly, washing his hands at the sink.

'In his study, I think.' She knew instinctively what he wanted him for. The testing time had arrived. She wondered whether there was any hope of appealing to his better nature and without giving herself time to think said:

'Damon, do you have to go through with this? Can't you see what a help I'll be to your father? He wants to finish his book, yet the housework takes up all his time. You admitted yourself you could get no one to take the work off his hands, so why not let me stay? It's the perfect solution.'

'Perfect for whom?' he asked stingingly. 'Yourself?' He flung down the towel with which he had been drying his hands. 'No, my mind's made up. If my father really wants a secretary I'll find someone who more suits the part.'

The thrust hurt. Corrie knew exactly what

107

he meant and he wasn't even giving her the chance to prove otherwise. 'How can you be so stubborn?' she cried, her square chin tilted defiantly. 'Don't you believe in giving anyone a fair chance?'

His grey eyes cut through her, coldly furious. 'Not anyone like you,' and the door whistled to a close, only to bang against the jamb and swing crazily open again.

Corrie's only hope now was Charles and she childishly crossed her fingers, hoping with all her heart that he would be able to persuade his son to keep her on.

She had not intended to listen but raised, angry voices echoed their way along the corridor, causing Corrie to alert every sense, straining now to hear what was being said. Anyone would do it under the circumstances, she excused herself, she could not be accused of eavesdropping, for their voices were loud enough to overhear.

'You're mistaken,' said Charles. 'The girl's not like that. You only have to look at her to—'

'To see that she's like her mother,' cut in Damon rudely. 'We have no way of knowing that she won't act like her and I don't want you upset again, Father. It's for your own good, can't you see that?'

A silence when Charles said something

108

quietly, and then Damon again, 'How do we know? How can we afford to take the risk? You've a soft spot for her already, given a few weeks she'll be taking over the place—ruling you too like Zelah did.'

'That's enough!'

Corrie had never heard Charles speak in that authoritative tone before, and a ray of hope ran through her.

'I still happen to love Zelah, despite what she's done. She's not all selfish and when she's ready to come back I shall take her.'

'You're an old fool.' Damon was really angry now. 'Don't you know she's taking you for a ride? Using your money, bleeding you—and you can't see it. God, Father, how can I make you see sense?'

'It's not my future we're discussing!' There was still a cold thread running through Charles' voice. 'It's that young girl out there, and I tell you, Damon, you're mistaken. She never knew her mother, how can you possibly say she's like her? Corrie's been brought up by a kind warm-hearted couple who love her as if she was their own, and against such a background no child will go off the rails. It was different for Zelah, she was left very much to her own devices when she was young, her parents didn't care what she did so long as she was out of their way. Now do you see why

109

I think she should be given this chance? No one can be accused without proof, Damon, no one, and I'm damn sure you're not going to talk me out of this now.'

It was not difficult to imagine Damon's reaction to this speech—disbelief, more anger, and a visible withdrawal from his father. His reply was too low for Corrie to hear, but a few seconds after that the door opened and heavy footsteps sounded on the tiled floor of the corridor.

Anxious not to be caught listening, Corrie hastened to the sink, turning on the tap and washing her hands. When the kitchen door closed and all she could hear behind her was a man's regular breathing she said, without turning, 'Well, Damon, what's the verdict? Am I in or out?'

But the voice that spoke was the deeper, more resonant one of his father. 'You're staying, child, I told you there would be no problem.'

Corrie spun round in relief and without hesitation flung herself into his arms. 'I'm so glad, I never thought you'd do it.'

He pressed her lips to her brow. 'You underestimate me. Once my mind's made up no one can dissuade me, not even that wilful son of mine!'

The door opened, but Corrie did not hear

it, she was so excited. 'Oh, I love you, Charles, I really do.'

'Is this the result you were hoping for, Father?' Damon's accusing voice cracked into the room like a whip. 'What a bloody fool I was to let you persuade me!'

He turned and was gone before either of them could speak. Corrie found her limbs were trembling so much that she was glad of Charles' supporting arm. Her eyes were moist as she looked up into his troubled blue ones. 'I'm sorry if I'm causing ill feelings,' she whispered. 'Perhaps it would be better, after all, if I went.'

'Nonsense,' asserted Charles firmly. 'He'll get over it.'

But despite his reassurance Corrie was worried. Although she desperately wanted to stay she did not want to be the cause of a rift between father and son, and it looked very much as though this was the way things were going.

She and Charles sat at the table and began to eat. 'I'll put Damon's dinner in the oven,' said Charles. 'He'll come in when he's good and ready, hungry as a horse.'

'Does he often miss his meals?' Corrie felt that she herself was to blame.

'He eats at odd hours,' smiled his father, 'but he certainly doesn't go without food.'

But when Corrie went to bed at ten-thirty Damon had still not returned to the house and she could not help feeling guilty. It was her fault that he had gone off in a rage—ought she to try and find him, perhaps make some sandwiches, because his dinner would surely be ruined. The thought of the rebuff she was almost certain to receive, though, made Corrie decide otherwise. Damon was man enough to look after himself, if he wanted to go hungry, let him.

The next morning, as soon as breakfast was cleared away, Charles suggested they make a start on his book. He had made an attempt to tidy his study, she noted with amusement, and the desk on which sat the typewriter was now clear of papers. The books on the floor still remained and the bookshelves were in need of being put into some sort of order, but the easy chair had gone and another desk taken its place.

He indicated the desk beneath the window. 'Sit down. I've been trying to sort things out.' He handed her a batch of papers, 'These are my earlier notes, if you could make a start on those. I thought that if I got them typed out in rough first then it would be a much simpler matter to put them into chronological order.'

Taking the cover from the typewriter she was relieved to find that it was a fairly recent model and in good order. 'Do you type?' she asked Charles, for all the notes appeared to be in long spidery writing.

He shook his head. 'Damon uses it sometimes, but the machine was bought specifically for when I got myself a secretary.'

'I see.' Satisfied but unable to imagine Damon sitting at a typewriter, Corrie inserted paper into the machine and started to type. Soon she became absorbed in the family history that unfolded before her eyes.

Charles' grandfather had been an O'Donovan and it was the O'Donovans who came to Ireland from Scotland in 1608 when James I was on the throne. They had settled in County Antrim but a few generations later moved south. Hawksmoor was built about 1728 and designed by a Sir Edward Lovett Pearce, apparently the most important Palladian architect of his day.

The O'Donovans were not a big family but had successfully built up their estate until they were one of the largest landowners in the district. It was during the famine of 1845–48 that one of the two remaining sons emigrated to America where he settled down and married. His own son, disliking America, had crossed to England. Charles' mother was born just before the turn of the century.

The last of the O'Donovans left in Ireland
113

had died some ten years ago, but it had taken several years to trace Charles Courtney and his son as the only surviving relatives.

'There are portraits of my antecedents at present stowed away until they can be hung,' Charles told her when she commented on this family tree he had discovered. 'I'll show them to you one day, you can definitely see the family resemblance.'

Charles' writing was difficult to read and by lunchtime Corrie was glad of the break. 'Will Damon be eating with us?' she enquired, as she sliced bread and placed it on the table with the cheese and pickles Charles had said he would like in preference to something cooked.

'It's anyone's guess.' He looked sad and Corrie could only presume that their argument was bothering him.

'I think I'll go and look for him,' she said, when the meal was ready and there was still no sign of him putting in an appearance.

Charles shrugged. 'I wouldn't worry your pretty head about my son, but if that's what you want, go ahead. You'll probably find him in the cowshed.'

Corrie was not worried about Damon missing another meal. He had breakfasted early, the remains being on the table when she herself got up, but it was his persistent rebuffal of his father that she did not like.

114

Charles was hurt by his son's attitude, that much she knew, even though he had said nothing to her, and this was the reason she wanted to talk to him now.

As she walked across the field towards the cowshed Corrie rehearsed what she was going to say, but, upon pushing open the door and as she saw the hard questioning face turned towards her, all thoughts fled. His attitude did not encourage conversation, least of all pleas on behalf of his father, but she knew she must try and hesitantly closed the door behind her and walked towards him.

'What do you want?' he asked harshly. 'Surely my father hasn't given you time off?'

'It's lunchtime,' she said, trying not to show how much his attitude hurt.

'I'm not hungry,' he returned, 'so if that's why you've come you're wasting your time.'

'That's not the reason.' She looked for the first time at the newly born calf attempting to struggle to its feet and ignoring Damon's hostility slid down to her knees in the straw beside him. 'Oh, isn't he beautiful? I've never seen a new-born calf before—he's gorgeous!'

The animal looked at her with big doleful eyes and Corrie wrapped her arms about him, cuddling the warm beast, for the moment forgetting Damon and the reason she was here.

It was Damon himself who interrupted this show of affection. 'Then why are you here? I haven't time to waste while you go into raptures over our latest addition. We have dozens like him every year.'

Corrie released the quivering brown and white animal and pushed herself to her feet, feeling a growing anger inside that he could be so insensitive. But she hadn't come here to argue, she had come to plead Charles' cause. 'It's your father,' she said abruptly.

'Is he ill?' frowned Damon instantly.

'No, no,' shaking her head, 'but I think you're treating him unfairly. I know I'm at the centre of it all and you can say what you like to me, it doesn't matter, but it does bother me to see Charles upset.'

'What's he been saying?' Damon hauled himself up, regarding her suspiciously.

Corrie had felt better with him on the floor, more in control of the situation. Now, compelled to look up at him, she felt at a disadvantage, but she stood her ground, saying firmly, 'He's said nothing, you should know he's not like that, but I can tell he's hurt. He hardly mentions you and when he does a shadow crosses his face that's not normally there.'

Damon shrugged, almost as though he did not care. 'He's a stubborn old cuss, he'll get over it.'

'Get over what?' demanded Corrie hotly, 'when you're making no attempt to patch up your argument. Okay, your father won, but why take it out on him? What's the matter, don't you like losing? Does it go against the grain to think that your father still has the say-so around here? He's not that old, you know.'

Curling his lips in contempt, Damon blazed, 'Not too old to make a good lover, is that what you mean?'

Corrie recoiled as though she had been struck, shocked that he should even think such a thing, yet alone voice his thoughts. 'How dare you!' she spat, every vestige of colour leaving her face.

'How dare I what?' he asked calmly. 'Say what I know to be the truth, or perhaps to be strictly accurate, to say what I know will be the inevitable conclusion of your relationship with my father? You forget I know him a great deal better than you.'

The insinuation brought tears to Corrie's eyes, burning hot tears that raced down her cheeks despite several attempts to stop them. She swallowed, angry with herself for revealing this weakness, but even more angry with Damon for suggesting that his father would—the thought alone flooded her cheeks with colour. Charles would never do such a

117

thing. He was honourable and looked upon her as his daughter. Their relationship was a new and wonderful thing and she did not intend to allow Damon's accusation to spoil it. 'Maybe you ought to question Charles about his feelings towards me? You could be in for a surprise.'

'Uh!' he scoffed. 'He wouldn't admit it. He probably doesn't even know yet. He sees only good in people, that's his trouble. Too soft by far is my father.'

'Perhaps it might pay you to take a leaf out of his book,' she flashed. 'At least he has faith in me. I don't see how you can judge a person by someone else's standards.'

'Are you pleading for yourself now?' he sneered, his ice-cold eyes regarding her with cruel insolence. 'Are you trying to convince me that you're not like your mother?' He took a step closer. 'It won't wash, and you know damn well it won't.'

Hard fingers caught her chin, painfully compelling her to look at him. He said slowly, menacingly, 'I could take you any time I want, and you know it. The only difference between you and Zelah is that she offered it to me.'

'You're a liar!' Anguished, Corrie tried in vain to pull free. 'You're making it up. I don't believe you, I won't believe you.' But the doubt had been planted in her mind and she knew it was just possible that he spoke the truth.

But for him to think that she was like Zelah! It was preposterous. It was that kiss that had done it, of course. Why had she let him? Why hadn't she struggled from the first instead of allowing the kiss to go on? She knew the answer. It had been a unique experience—and a pleasurable one, she could not deny it, but she would refute the fact that she threw herself at any man who happened along. Her eyes blazing with hatred she pummelled his chest, but for all the effect it had she might have been beating her hands against a brick wall.

Damon laughed harshly and caught her wrists, imprisoning them both in one giant brown hand, his other reaching up to brush back the silky white hair that had fallen across her face.

She stiffened, as his fingers stroked her cheek, remaining there a moment, setting her nerves quivering.

His eyes dared her to deny that his touch had no effect. In the shadows of the cowshed they appeared a darker grey and the harsh plane of his face had softened. Or was that her imagination? Had the fact that her pulses were racing faster than normal also made her see things that were not there? Was this what she

119

wanted? A Damon who had relented, found her desirable? 'No!' she cried aloud, shaking her head. This wasn't what she wanted at all. This man was a hateful, detestable beast, and she wanted to be free of him.

'No, what?' he asked in a softly menacing tone. 'No, you don't want me to touch you, or are you trying to tell yourself that you shouldn't give in to those impulses which are even now springing to life inside your beautiful body?' His hand, which had fallen free as she moved her head, came to rest on her shoulder, his thumb sensuously stroking the base of her throat.

A strangled cry of protest broke from Corrie. 'You swine, let me go!' But in answer he merely laughed and tightened his fingers round her wrists, pulling her even closer so that their bodies touched and she could feel the power of his limbs; inflexible, iron-hard. What point was there in trying to fight him? He was certain to win. What was it he wanted from her—another submission, another victory gained? Or more proof that she was the type of person he had classed her?

Even as these thoughts flitted through her mind, her own body was a traitor. The feel of this man's thighs against her own, even under such extenuating circumstances, was sufficient to build up fires within her breast, setting her vibrantly alive and very much in danger of losing control of the situation.

She closed her eyes. It was imperative that she shut out that harsh face, shut out altogether this man who was becoming far too dangerous for her peace of mind.

But when his hand slid down the open neck of her blouse, not so gently now, but urgent in its caress of her gently rounded breasts, Corrie's eyes shot open, made large with offended dignity, and lowering her head she sank her teeth into his wrist, not relaxing until he jerked back in pain.

'You little bitch,' he grated, 'you're not going to get away with that!' His eyes had narrowed, masking the silver glitter, but his nostrils flared and tightened lips told their own story.

With little thought whether he might hurt her he pushed Corrie down on to the straw beside the startled calf. The young animal huddled up to its mother who was mooing in protest of this disturbance in her stall. Damon then threw himself on top of her, pinning her arms above her head, and pressing his hard lips to hers, savagely demanding a response.

Corrie knew that if she dared to relax he would get it—she had to fight herself as well as him. Using all her strength, she tossed her head from side to side and he was forced to release her hands so that he could steady her face.

She became aware of the urgency building up inside Damon, heightened no doubt by the feel of her body beneath him, and her own breathing became ragged, her senses drugged by this thing that was bigger than herself.

She liked the feel of his body on hers, it was as though they were melting into one another. Had she not been in absolute control of her emotions she knew that she would have wound her arms round his head and run her fingers through that thick black hair.

His mouth moved on hers, sensuous, demanding, parting her lips. A heady lightness welled up inside her and it was all she could do to remain impassive, pretend that his embrace had no effect. In reality she wanted to throw away her defences and give herself up with glorious abandon to the exquisite pleasure of his embrace.

His kisses were like nothing else she had ever experienced; expert, intense, passionate, trying hard to draw some response, and she had to curl her fists into a tight ball and steel her body not to give in. The desire was there. Whatever else Damon Courtney might have wrong with him he certainly knew how to make love. It made her wonder, with his aversion to women, from where he had gained his experience, and whether he would remain a bachelor all his life, perhaps using women as he was using her now, to relieve his pent-up emotions.

The weakness that assailed her limbs threatened to be her downfall. It was only by sheer determination that she was able to withstand his assault on her senses and when he finally stopped, rolling away from her before pushing himself to his feet, she could not move. She felt drained, utterly incapable of finding the strength to lift herself up.

She was aware that he looked down, though his expression for the moment escaped her. Her eyes were misted by unshed tears. She felt ashamed that she had enjoyed his touch to the extent that she had almost broken down. The only redeeming factor was that she had managed to remain firm, but even so she felt humiliated and wondered again whether she had inherited some of her mother's make-up.

It was possible, yet she had never felt like it before, not with John, not with anyone. It was only this man who was able to stir up an emotion which hitherto she had been unaware of. His expertise had stimulated physical desires which were foreign to her, not unpleasant, but frightening. It was embarrassing to think that she might have given in to this despicable man. Thank goodness she hadn't, the degradation would have been too much to bear.

'Are you going to lie there all day?' he asked finally. 'Is it an invitation that you're ready for more, or have my kisses robbed you of your senses?'

This latter was too near the truth for her liking, but it had the desired effect. Corrie shot to her feet, her cheeks flaming and her pretty blue eyes glaring crossly. 'I hope you're proud of yourself,' she said distantly. 'What a pity it didn't have the result you expected.'

'It told me a great deal about you,' he said, and she noticed that he was smiling, apparently not in the least disturbed by her lack of response. 'I know for instance that you were not as immune to me as you made out. A little more—persuasion—and you would have been mine.'

'Like hell I would,' she snapped. 'No girl in her right mind would allow a beast like you to make love to her.' She smoothed her skirt. 'I'd better get back. Your father will be wondering what's happened.'

'What will you tell him, I wonder?' he mused, his eyes glittering oddly. 'The truth? That his son attempted to rape you on the cowshed floor? Or will you conjure up some neat little lie designed to protect him from harsh realities?'

124

'It would serve you right if I did tell him,' she bit back, 'but I don't suppose I will. I'll save you the humiliation.'

'It wouldn't bother me.' His thumbs were hooked into the top of his jeans, his legs slightly apart and his head tilted to one side, studying her intently. 'It must be your own face you're trying to save. If so I suggest you pull that straw out of your hair. You could have difficulty in explaining how it got there.'

Ignoring the jibe, Corrie removed the straw, running her fingers through her hair to make sure there was no more.

'You've still missed some,' he said. 'Would you like me to get it out for you?' He took a step nearer, his hand already raised, but Corrie backed away.

'I can manage,' she said sharply. For him to approach her again would be more than she could endure. Even now she was intensely aware of his virile strength, and the remembrance of those hard-muscled limbs against her own caused her heart beats to quicken their pace once more.

'I don't want you to touch me—not ever again,' she said, her voice breaking, and let herself out of the shed to run all the way back to the house.

CHAPTER SEVEN

Corrie thought that Charles gave her a strange look when she re-entered the house, but he said nothing, for which she was grateful, and after their lunch they spent the whole afternoon in the study. So engrossed did she become in the work that it was with reluctance she stopped when Charles declared it was time to call it a day.'

'I'll prepare dinner,' he said. 'You go and get some fresh air.'

'I'd rather help,' she pleaded, knowing she would feel guilty doing nothing while he worked. After all, they had both been hard at it all day.

But Charles insisted and Corrie found herself left to her own devices. Deciding to steer clear of the cowshed in case Damon was still somewhere in the area, she walked down into the valley towards where she could see the still waters of a lake sparkling in the early evening sunshine.

Her path took her through open fields and a beech copse, breaking out suddenly into an open space where immediately before her was the lake she had sought. Hardly a ripple broke its surface, the silken expanse of water reflected to perfection the fir and beech on its far banks, the blue of the sky, even a bird which hovered above almost as though it was watching her, wondering what she was doing here in this valley which belonged to the Courtneys.

Was it a hawk? she mused, her mind winging back over the years to the O'Donovans who had given this valley its name. In some peculiar way Damon reminded her of a hawk, with his proud bearing, his very slightly hooked nose. She, at the moment, was his prey, though as yet he had not managed to get his talons into her. He had striven to drive her out of Ireland without success and she pondered on what his next move would be.

She could not believe he had given up the attempt, despite the fact that his father had been adamant in his decision that she stay. So what would Damon do now? Perhaps make life so impossible that she would want to leave? It could have been the reason behind that attempted love scene earlier. She went hot at the thought. Did it mean that each time they were alone he would try to make love? Was this now to be his method of attack, believing that she would either succumb, thus proving him right, or she would so heartily despise his advances that she would be glad to go?

Her lips firmed resolutely. She would do neither. If he attempted to kiss her she would evade him, politely but firmly. In that way she would be in complete control of herself with no possible danger that her reactions would give him a lever with which to hit back.

She turned, intending to retrace her steps, but as if to test this newly formed resolution Damon himself approached. At first she toyed with the idea of pretending she had not seen him, of taking a roundabout route back to the house, but then she logically decided that he would know what she was doing—most probably exult in the effect he was having upon her. So she walked bravely towards him, forcing her small sensitive lips to smile, even though she was in no way pleased.

'You surprise me,' he said by way of greeting. 'Why are you not cooking dinner?'

Her blue eyes narrowed, knowing full well that he was trying to get her going. 'I was not aware that that was one of my jobs,' she said primly. 'So far as I know I'm only being paid to help with your father's writing.' She could have told him that Charles had adamantly refused her offer of help, but why should she? Let him think what he liked, it mattered not to her.

'So,' came his cutting response, 'you prefer

to let my father work doubly hard while you yourself relax and enjoy the beauty of our valley.'

When Corrie made no reply he continued, 'Another of Zelah's traits coming out in her daughter. She was like that, did you know? Considered housework beneath her, tried to be a lady.' He sniffed. 'She would never be that in a million years.'

Although Corrie had up to yet heard no good of her mother she resented Damon speaking ill of her. Her eyes flashed as she said, 'I don't think you're being fair. I'm sure Zelah was not all bad, there must have been some good in her for Charles to love her.'

'Father's in his dotage. I excuse him, but I don't excuse you, and I don't like the idea of him being taken advantage of.'

'Who's taking advantage?' queried Corrie with assumed innocence.

'He's taken you in out of the goodness of his heart,' he stormed, 'you could have the common decency to help out with the housework.'

'I don't see you lending a hand,' she retorted heatedly, wishing she had never allowed this farcical conversation to begin.

'My time's taken up running the estate, as you well know, and if my father's going to work eight hours a day on his book I don't

129

want him doing all the work in the house as well. Understood?'

'Perfectly,' Corrie kept her voice icily polite, 'but if I have anything to do with the cooking of the meals I shall expect you there on time to eat them. I don't like wasting food.'

'Are you trying to give me orders?'

The dangerous glitter in his eyes should have warned Corrie not to continue, but heedless she said, 'If you like to take it that way. Regular meal times would be best for all of us. I suspect your father neglected himself, if we all eat together he'll have no excuse.'

Fortunately for her this reference to Charles appeared to do the trick and his face relaxed. 'You could be right. I'll try, but you must realise that sometimes it's impossible for me to get away.'

'I appreciate that,' she replied with quiet dignity. 'Now, if you'll excuse me, I'll go and see if Charles needs a hand.' She did not mind the fact that Damon thought he had won, that her decision to help had been because of his intervention. She didn't care what he thought about her, or so she kept telling herself. She had to, otherwise she would be hurt by his attitude. In actual fact it mattered very much what Damon thought and she resented his continued references to her mother.

She hoped they were not really the same

130

because there was nothing more she wanted than for Damon to like her—no, love her, as she loved him! For the first time she admitted it to herself, John temporarily forgotten. As she walked back towards the house, listening to his feet following, scuffling through the decaying leaves of last autumn, she knew without a shadow of doubt that she loved Damon.

It was a heart-stopping thought and probably a futile one, for there seemed little likelihood that he would ever return her feelings. Damon Courtney struck her as the sort of man who, once he had made up his mind about a person, would have difficulty in changing that opinion, and she was the last person with whom he was capable of falling in love.

She paused, waiting for him to catch her up, ignoring his swift interrogative glance. 'Are you coming back to the house too?'

He nodded. 'I've finished for today, thought I'd spend an evening with my father. He likes a game of chess and it's been a long time since we played.'

Corrie had no difficulty in guessing the motive behind this decision. It was blatantly obvious that he was doing it so that she herself would not be alone with Charles, other than when they were working. In his own devious way Damon was attempting to put a stop to the relationship which, if he only knew, was all a figment of his imagination. Her feelings for Charles went no deeper than any daughter for her father, not even that deep perhaps, for she was as yet not fully acquainted with the man.

'It's not a game I've ever played,' she said, wondering if he would offer to teach her.

But all he said was, 'A pity,' not sounding in the least sorry, 'but I've no doubt you'll be able to find something to occupy your time. You could even get on with my father's book, the quicker it's finished the sooner you can go back home.'

'You'd like that, wouldn't you?' she accused. 'But so far as I can see it will take a long, long time. His facts are all a jumble, they have to be sorted and sifted and then written into some acceptable form. It can't be done in a matter of weeks. It will take months, perhaps even a year.'

Damon did not like that and frowned swiftly. 'I'm not sure I believe you. My father's been working on it for goodness knows how long. Are you sure you're not trying to stretch out the work just so that you can stay? I wouldn't advise you to do that.'

Corrie shrugged and looked obliquely at the man striding along beside her. 'Why not, it won't affect you? In fact I would say it will make your life a lot easier if I take over part of the running of the house as well. Don't you agree?'

'The heck I don't,' he growled. He said no more, but the stern expression on his face told her that he was not at all happy with the situation.

They went round the back of the house and into the kitchen, Corrie humming happily. Charles was there and looked up, returning her smile warmly. 'Enjoyed your walk, my dear? You're back sooner than I expected.'

'She's come to help.' Damon pushed into the kitchen behind her. 'I don't agree with her relaxing while you do all the work.'

'It was my idea,' returned Charles calmly. 'She's already offered, but never mind, Corrie, now you're here you can make the custard. You're much better at it than me.'

Corrie smiled and took a bottle of milk from the fridge, ignoring Damon who was frowning strongly as though the situation puzzled him.

After dinner the men retired to the sitting room to play their game of chess and Corrie remained behind to deal with the washing up. In one respect she was glad Damon had offered to spend the evening with his father, even though his prime purpose had been to spite herself and not out of any feeling of duty.

Charles, however, was not aware of this. He knew that his son was against her remaining, but he did not know the extent of Damon's antagonism. She guessed he would be angry if he knew, declaring that he had no foundation on which to base his dislike. He would not accept that her relationship with Zelah was sufficient. She herself had heard him telling Damon that her upbringing alone would have a bearing on her nature.

Take Damon and Charles, for instance. They looked alike, but that was as far as it went. In every other respect they were opposites, so why then could Damon not accept that she was different from her mother? It would mean a great deal to her if he could. She had done nothing to give him cause for distrust, nothing at all. Unless one counted those incidents when they first met. She herself had long forgotten them. Now, in retrospect, they seemed trivial and nothing upon which this man could reasonably found his suspicions.

Her lips were trembling by the time she had finished tidying the kitchen. It would mean so much to her, Damon's friendship, even though she knew it would be treading on dangerous ground.

There was John to consider too, and she felt guilty when she realised how far from her

134

mind he had become; she scarcely thought of him these days. It was Damon who occupied her thoughts. Surprising really, considering the way he treated her, but love was like that, she told herself, coming at the most unexpected times and in the most unlikely places.

She realised now that the feelings she had had for John were not love. She liked him very much, as a friend, but that was as far as it went. His kisses had had no fire in them, had not aroused the burning desire which Damon's slightest touch could evoke. In fact Damon had only to look at her to set her pulses racing. Even now, at the mere thought of him, she had gone warm and her fingers involuntarily touched her lips where his kisses had burned just a few hours ago.

The attraction was not entirely physical either. It played a great part, but she knew that she also found Damon attractive in other ways. He could be a great friend, an adviser, a companion—all of these as well as a superb lover.

A shattering combination, but he was a shattering man. It would be difficult persuading him that she was not the harlot he thought—but worth while. It would be up to her to prove her case. By not one word or deed must she give him reason to believe her

135

anything other than pure—which she was, of course, except that it seemed Damon Courtney was not prepared to believe it.

Once the kitchen was clean and tidy she joined the men, sitting on one of the gold brocade chairs, not too near to disturb them but not too far away so that she could not watch their game. But she found that her eyes were frequently drawn to Damon's face rather than the pieces on the board. He was concentrating, seemingly oblivious of her presence, and although she knew none of the techniques she guessed that both men were equal and needed all their skill and determination if they were to win.

In profile it was easier to see the resemblance between father and son. Both had the same hooked nose and high broad forehead, even their lips were set in the same firm lines and the look of ferocious concentration set their faces into harsh lines. Corrie loved them both, but for very different reasons.

'Stalemate,' announced Charles at length when the silence in the room had grown so tangible that Corrie had been almost afraid to breathe.

Damon laughed. 'I'll beat you yet. Another game?'

But Charles shook his head. 'I think we

ought to entertain our guest. She's been very patient sitting there while we finished our game. Do you play, Corrie?' and when she shook her head, 'Perhaps Damon will teach you.'

'I don't think I'd enjoy it,' she said, before the younger man could speak. 'I like something with a bit of go in it. I play a lot of squash and tennis.'

'I'm afraid we have no facilities for anything like that.' Damon sounded condescending. 'If that's what you're after then this quiet corner of Ireland is not for you.'

'It's not what I want,' proclaimed Corrie, 'I was just saying what I liked. There's no harm in that, is there?'

Charles broke in tactfully, 'I'm afraid Damon misunderstood you. How about a drink? Is Irish whiskey all right, or do you find it a little too potent?'

'I've never tried it,' she said honestly, 'just a drop, with some water, I think.'

Damon packed away the chessmen while Charles poured the drinks and when they were all seated the older man said, 'It's very pleasant, the three of us together like this. It's been a long time since we had such a charming companion, don't you agree, Damon?'

Damon gave her a long considering look before he spoke. 'You're entitled to your

137

opinion, Father. I prefer to reserve my judgment.'

Corrie flushed, almost hating him for being so rude to her in front of Charles.

His father frowned, 'I thought you'd got over that silly idea. It's preposterous! You only have to look at Corrie to see innocence written all over her face. You've misjudged her, Damon, why don't you admit it?'

'Have I, Father? What proof have you?'

'None but what I can see with my own eyes and what I can feel in my bones.' Charles looked at Corrie, noting her signs of distress. 'Look what you're doing to the child, see how upset she is. Shame on you, Damon!'

'I'm sorry,' said Damon, without the slightest indication that he was. 'Do forgive me.'

It satisfied his father, but she knew that he had not meant it and wondered just what she would have to do to prove herself. It would take a long time, probably the whole length of her stay, and even then he might not change his opinion of her. She squared her shoulders. All she could do was try—and to begin with she must show that his animosity in no way hurt.

So she said, pretending to accept his apology, 'That's all right, Damon. I know you can't help believing what you want. Let's

138

hope you'll change your mind before I go home.'

'Why?' he asked abruptly. 'Does it bother you what I think?'

She shrugged. 'Why should it? I'm working for your father, not you. I couldn't care less what you think.' She had not meant to tack on these last few words, but somehow his attitude destroyed all her good intentions. He thought he was so superior, so perfect, when in fact his faults were as great as those he attributed to herself. He was guilty of thinking the worst of her, without cause, and this rankled, so much so that she almost felt like backing down and going home. But she wouldn't, of course. Running away would solve nothing.

'I'm glad to hear it,' he said, 'because it would make no difference. Once my mind's made up about a person, it's very rarely I change it. Unless I'm proved wrong, of course, and then I would apologise.'

This Corrie would like to see—Damon apologising! How highly improbable it sounded. She would not be surprised if he had never made an apology in his life.

'You might find you have to do that before long,' intervened Charles. 'It's not often I disagree with you, son, but on this score I most definitely do. I'm on Corrie's side all the way.'

139

'Thank you, Charles,' she said, smiling warmly at him. 'You're a dear.'

'And what am I, an ogre?' growled Damon, clearly disliking this display of affection between his father and the girl he considered to be no better than her mother.

'You're acting like one,' said Charles, frowning. 'I've never seen you like this before and I can't imagine why.'

'I think you do,' replied Damon. 'You just refuse to accept it. But I can see your point of view, even though I don't agree, so please don't bother yourself on my behalf.'

'It's Corrie who concerns me,' Charles looked across at her, smiling in a comforting sort of way, as if to say, never mind, I'm on your side, even if Damon isn't. 'I'm sure she doesn't deserve your rudeness. Why don't you accept her at face value? At least make her stay with us pleasant. We don't want her going home with unhappy memories.'

To her surprise Damon said, 'Very well, Father, if it will make you happy. But that's my only reason.'

There was nothing else that Charles could say, but he appeared satisfied. Corrie herself doubted Damon would keep to his word, but it would be nice if he did. It was the chance she needed to prove to him once and for all the type of girl she was.

140

For the next few days it seemed that Damon really was trying. He appeared promptly at all meal times and during the evenings when the three of them were together he showed none of his earlier animosity, treating her almost as a sister.

This was not exactly what Corrie had wanted, but at least it was better than having him perpetually warring. He even offered to teach her to play chess, but after a few games she gave up. The game was too slow and required too much concentration for her liking.

Occasionally they went for walks in the valley, and it was at times like this that Corrie felt acutely aware of the power Damon held over her. His physical magnetism was like an invisible string drawing her ever closer. John faded deeper and deeper into the background and Damon began to take over all her waking and sleeping thoughts. She rarely felt guilty; it seemed natural somehow, as though Damon was the person for whom she had been waiting all her life.

She only wished that his feelings for her were different. Since that time he had kissed her in the cowshed he had made no further advances, not even so much as holding her hand when they were out walking, though sometimes she had caught him looking at her

141

in an entirely incomprehensible way.

It was on one evening such as this when they had walked as far as the lake and the stillness of twilight was all about them, casting a magical spell, that Corrie voiced the question which had been in her mind for sometime now.

'Damon!' She paused, waiting until she had his full attention. 'Do you—I mean, are you still of the same opinion—about me?'

He leaned back against the trunk of a tree, almost melting into the shadows that were stealing all about them. 'Is there any reason why I shouldn't be?' he asked, making her feel as though it had been a pointless question.

'These last few days,' she persisted, 'haven't they meant anything to you? Haven't they proved I'm not—what you think I am?' She stood close to him, too close really for comfort because the familiar quickening of her heart threatened to make itself loud enough to be overheard, but she wanted to be near enough to see his expression.

His dark gaze rested on her face, searching, penetrating, reducing her nerves to quivering emotion. 'You've behaved exactly as I expected—for someone who's out to prove they're what they're not.'

'But that's where you're wrong,' said Corrie desperately. 'This is me, the real me. I'm not

142

what you think, truly I'm not.'

'Because you haven't had the chance? Cooped up here with my father and me there's no one to impress with your silver hair and pretty-pretty face.'

Corrie stamped her foot angrily. 'Sometimes I hate you! You say the most despicable things! If anyone's been acting, it's you. All this week you've been nice to me, but it's all been a lie. You feel no differently now from that day we first met.'

His arms were folded across his chest and now he tilted his head to one side. 'I thought you knew that.' He sounded amused. 'I'm doing it for my father's sake, not yours.'

'And I thought we were getting somewhere.' Corrie did not realise how wistful she sounded.

'Poor Corrie,' he mocked. 'Do you really mind? Does a person like you have a heart so that it matters what people think? Or is it the fact that I haven't succumbed to your obvious beauty like all the other men with whom you come into contact?' He was no longer amused. His eyes glittered harshly in the fading light, the planes of his face had never seemed to angular, his lips so condemning.

Corrie could have cried. At last, when she had felt she was getting somewhere, she now discovered that his kindness had been a

143

façade. She should have known. He had told his father he would be nice to her purely to make him happy, but somehow, idiot that she was, she had gained the impression that it had been no hardship. He had even seemed to enjoy her company. How gullible she had been!

'No matter what I say,' she returned hotly, 'you won't believe me. I was a fool for even thinking you might change your mind. Forget I said anything.'

She turned away, determined he should not see the tears that were forcing their way beneath her lashes. But he caught her roughly by the shoulder. 'Wait, there had to be a reason behind your question. I want to know what it was.'

'Because I love you,' she could have said. That would have been a laugh. She meant nothing to him, nothing more than a nuisance he was compelled to endure for his father's sake, and anyway it was highly improbable he would believe her. He would see it as her way of attempting to get him into her clutches. He no doubt thought she regarded him as a challenge, one man who had not fallen for her instantly. 'I don't have to tell you,' she said.

'No, you don't,' he admitted readily, 'but I think I know. You're piqued because I haven't paid you more attention, isn't that it?'

Just as she had thought. She sighed deeply before saying, 'I didn't expect you to. You make no secret of the fact that you despise me. I was just hoping—futilely as it turns out—that you might have revised your opinion.'

'And it was important enough for you to ask, knowing the risk you took of me being nasty to you?'

'I've grown used to that, it doesn't bother me any more.'

'Then why are you trembling, if you're not afraid?'

This was a question she could not answer—not without admitting her true feelings. But how could you explain to a man who detested you that his touch caused a whirlpool of emotion, a longing to feel his arms about you and his kisses burning your lips? It was a laughable situation really, if she felt like laughing, but she didn't. She wanted to cry, to let the pent-up tears flow and draw her strength from the arms of this man.

He tilted her chin with one finger. 'Corrie, answer me.' And then he saw her tears, and frowned. 'You are afraid—unless—' suspicion took the place of surprise, 'those tears are false? A ruse designed to play on my compassion. It's a pity I have none.' His voice hardened and now he shook her violently. 'You don't move me, you slut. Feeling

145

frustrated, are you, after a week spent in almost monastic seclusion? You need to feel a man's arms about you, the assurance that you're still an attractive woman? You are that,' he said thickly, his arms tightening about her waist. 'Far too attractive for any man's peace of mind.'

His mouth claimed hers despite her cry of protest. His kiss was brutally punishing, harsh and savage, but filling her with an insane desire for more. She could not stop her arms curling round his neck, or her body straining against him, acutely aware of his rising passion.

'Is this what you want?' he demanded gruffly, lifting his mouth momentarily, his grey eyes blazing into the luminous blue of her own. 'Is this what you were after in your roundabout sort of way? Why didn't you ask me outright, I'd have been willing to oblige.' His breathing became ragged as his hands explored her body, his mouth forcing her lips apart.

Corrie wanted to deny him, to wrench away from his demanding hands and mouth, but some inner force, stronger than herself, made her respond and with total abandon she gave herself up to the pleasure of the moment.

CHAPTER EIGHT

Had Damon not flung her from him in disgust Corrie did not know what might have happened. She had completely lost control of herself, conscious only of a desire to be possessed by this man. Pride had deserted her and she felt no shame in clinging to his hard impassioned body, her lips melting beneath his, scarcely heeding the savage ferocity with which he took her.

The experience was shattering, leaving her in no doubt that she did truly love Damon and wanted nothing more than to be loved by him, to be treated as his most coveted possession. No one had ever told her that physical contact between a man and a woman could be like this, completely denuding her of all other senses except the need to feel his mouth ravaging her senses and his hands caressing her body.

When he let her go she stumbled backwards, her legs so weak that she fell sprawling across the grass. Her eyes, when she looked up at him, were wide with hurt dignity and she was about to protest when Damon himself spoke:

'Another time I won't be so lenient. I abhor

147

shameless women. How can you deny that you're not like Zelah when you throw yourself at me exactly as she used to?'

Corrie scrambled to her feet, her eyes blazing, all passion knocked from her body by his harsh words. 'It's not true, you're only saying that to hurt me!'

'Oh, but it is. She wasn't satisfied with my father alone. She needed a stronger, more virile man to fulfil her insatiable appetite.'

'If you responded,' cried Corrie, 'then you're no better than she, but I won't have you comparing me with her. There's no comparison. Haven't you learned that by now? I didn't ask you to kiss me, you started it, so why do I get the blame?'

'You could have tried stopping me,' he said caustically. 'It would be the obvious response if you didn't want me to touch you.' He paused, his eyes narrowing before he continued, 'But no, you wanted me—as much as I want you.' Shocked surprise on Corrie's face made him stop again. 'Oh, yes,' he concluded. 'I want you. You're very desirable—too much so for my peace of mind.'

'So that's the real reason you want me to go?' put in Corrie quickly. 'It's yourself you can't trust.'

'Don't be misguided.' The dark eyes never

left her face. 'I'm in perfect control of myself. My concern is for my father. After all, you're shut up with him for hours on end every day. Who knows what might happen? He's a full-blooded male like myself and no man is ever too old to appreciate a beautiful woman.'

Corrie felt like kicking his teeth in. His continued innuendoes about Charles and herself sickened her. 'You're contemptible! I don't know why I bother to talk to you. Every time you say something designed to hurt me.'

'Your conscience bothering you?' he mocked. 'You surprise me. I thought your type had no feelings.'

'There you go again!' she yelled angrily. 'Can't you understand I'm an ordinary decent girl who up till now has led an ordinary decent life?'

'Really! Then I must be the greatest disbeliever in the world, because I still think you're shooting me a pack of lies.'

Darkness had closed in around them as they argued and it was almost impossible now to read his face. Corrie could well imagine, though, the insolence with which he regarded her, the mockery in those dark eyes, and she was filled with a hatred almost as intense as the love she had felt only minutes earlier.

She curled her fingers into her palms, longing to lash out, but realising the futility of such an action. Instead she tilted her chin and said with as much dignity as she could muster, 'I feel sorry for you, Damon. Such a narrow-minded attitude must be restricting.' She walked away and this time he did not follow.

Corrie went straight up to her room when she reached the house, glad that Charles was nowhere in sight. The battle had left her both mentally and physically exhausted and she flung herself down on to the bed, only now allowing the tears to fall freely.

Why, oh, why, she asked herself time and time again, had she fallen in love with someone as hateful as Damon? There was no comparison between him and John. If only she had kept a hold on her former love none of this would have happened.

Not until now did it occur to her that she ought to write to John; explain her feelings and say that there was no point in him coming over. It would be a difficult letter but one perhaps best done now, while she was in this cold condemning mood, when there would be no fear that her feelings for Damon would creep into her writing.

She felt sorry for John. It would be a shock, but there was no point in continuing their relationship feeling as she did. It would be as distressing to marry a man she did not love as not being able to marry the man she did.

Her mind made up she went down to the study and began her letter. It was difficult and she had made several attempts when the door opened and Damon came in.

He looked surprised to see her alone and Corrie said, 'What's the matter? Did you expect to find me here with your father? Did you think I might have been crying on his shoulder, telling him what sort of a bully you are?'

'It wouldn't surprise me,' he said coldly. 'What are you doing, not working, surely?'

'I'm writing to John,' she said, 'though I don't see what business it is of yours.'

His face lightened, 'Ah, the lonely lover. Did our little—er—session, jog your conscience?' His eyes dropped to the wastepaper basket. 'By the look of it it's a difficult letter,' and before she could stop him he bent and retrieved one of the screwed-up sheets.

'Give that to me,' she cried, 'it's private! You have no right—' But already he had straightened the paper and ran his eyes over the tell-tale sentences.

He frowned and looked at her. 'A change of heart. Why?'

'It has nothing to do with Charles if that's what you're thinking,' she defended hotly. 'I've had time to think things over, that's all,

151

though I don't see why I should tell you. It's none of your concern.'

'If your coming here has anything to do with it, it concerns me a great deal,' Damon returned, his brow still furrowed. He folded the paper carefully before handing it back to her. 'I should be careful what you say, unless you want him to come hotfooting it over here to find out what's wrong.'

'He's coming anyway,' she told him. 'Your father's invited him. Didn't he tell you? My letter was designed to stop him.'

'It won't do that,' he said, 'not if the man thinks anything of you. Perhaps it might not be such a bad thing after all. It will keep you in place, if nothing else.'

Corrie glared. 'I wasn't aware that I'd stepped out of line.'

'No?' The raised eyebrows told her what he thought of that remark. 'You surprise me. I would think about that if I were you. Meantime I'll leave you to get on with your—difficult letter. Goodnight, Corrie.'

She did not answer. It was impossible to have the last word where Damon was concerned.

After his interruption she found it even more difficult to word her letter and in the end she gave up and went to bed. But sleep evaded her. Damon's kisses had had a deeper effect than she cared to admit and she could not help wondering what the future held in store.

She had to constantly remind herself that the reason she was here was Charles. He was the one who needed her—and she needed him. His sane assurances and his belief in her comforted Corrie when his son was at his most merciless. If it was not for Charles she doubted whether she could stick it out. Damon could be heartlessly cruel when he chose and there were not many occasions when he relented sufficiently to be nice to her.

★　　　★　　　★

For the next few days Corrie kept out of Damon's way as much as possible, spending more hours than was really necessary working on his father's book, to the extent that most evenings now she was in the study while the two men played chess or sat talking in the sitting room.

More than once Charles tried to persuade her to join them, but she was adamant in her refusal, and Damon did not even bother to try. She had not expected him to, but even so it hurt that he thought so little of her company that her absences bothered him not at all.

She had now written her letter to John and daily expected a reply. She tried to put herself

153

in his position and wondered what his reaction would be. Would he, as Damon said, hurry over to find out what had gone wrong, or would he wait until she returned to try and sort things out between them?

On the other hand he might write and demand that she pack up this job and go back home immediately. He had never been the sort to give orders, usually allowing Corrie to go her own way. But this was different. It all depended on whether he thought there was another man involved. She had made no mention of Damon, merely stating that she was working for Charles, but that while she had been away she had had time to think things over and had decided that marriage between them would not work out. She hoped he would understand and would discuss it fully when her work here was finished and she returned to Walsall.

With Charles she had no problems. They got on well and a deep bond had developed between them. He looked upon her as a daughter and treated her with as much love and kindness as if she had indeed been his own flesh and blood. She grew to love him dearly too, though never for one moment did she forget Anne and David who had devoted their life to bringing her up. She wrote regularly to them, always keeping her letters

154

bright and cheerful and full of the work she was doing.

She made no reference to Zelah and Anne was too discreet to mention her herself—no doubt relieved, thought Corrie, that she had apparently given up her search. In fact it was very rarely that she herself thought about Zelah these days. Charles did not mention her and she did not see enough of Damon to get into conversation with him. If she had—well, it went without saying that he would take great delight in comparing the two of them.

It was half way through her second week when Corrie, going down to breakfast, found that Charles was missing. Normally they ate together, it was most unusual for him not to be there with the breakfast ready or at least half cooked. Perhaps he was sleeping in, she thought, as she switched on the cooker and began to prepare their meal herself. But when at half past nine he had still not put in an appearance she decided to go up to his room and make sure he was all right.

Each day she made his bed and kept the room tidy. He had objected at first, but soon accepted her help happily. Now she tapped on the door and when there was no answer walked in. Charles was just getting out of bed, his eyes bleary with sleep. 'Oh, Corrie, I'm sorry, I appear to have overslept.'

155

Relieved that there was nothing wrong, Corrie laughed. 'I was worried about you— thought you might be ill or something.'

'Nothing more than a headache,' he said. 'I woke early and took some aspirins, must have dropped off again. Unlike me to sleep late, as you well know.'

He looked pale and Corrie said, 'Are you sure you're all right? You don't look your usual self. Why don't you stay in bed this morning? I'll bring your breakfast up, it's ready.'

Charles hesitated. 'That would be nice. It's been a long time since I indulged myself, but—'

'Then that's settled,' she cut in immediately. 'I won't be a moment.'

She left the room before he could think up an excuse and carefully arranged his tray. He had climbed back into bed when she returned, making Corrie think that he really must be feeling poorly, for normally nothing would keep him in bed.

But he ate his bacon and eggs with relish while Corrie sat at his side and talked about his book and the work she intended doing that day. 'There's enough to keep me going without you,' she said, 'so don't feel guilty lying here. It will do you good.'

She washed up and then went into the study

and began to type. Charles' writing had always been difficult to read, but usually she managed. However, after about half an hour's work she could make no sense of one particular passage and knew she would have to go up and ask him to translate.

'I'm sorry to disturb you,' she apologised, as she entered his room, 'but I'm stuck.'

As she had known, Charles did not mind and even said something about getting up. He soon sorted out her problem and she was smiling at her own stupidity in being unable to understand it when she left his room.

Damon was outside, a black frown darkening his brow. 'What the hell are you playing at?' he demanded angrily. 'Why were you in my father's room?'

'I was asking him something about his book,' she said, holding up the papers so that he could see for himself.

'A likely story,' he sneered. 'I must have been a fool to leave you in the house with him day after day. How long's this been going on?'

Corrie looked at him in total amazement. 'How long's what—you surely don't still think that we—that Charles and I are—no, it's too ridiculous for words!'

'I don't think so,' he said stiffly. 'I suspected it from the beginning, but I gave you the benefit of the doubt, not thinking you'd be blatant enough to do it under my very nose.'

Tilting her chin defiantly, and still confounded by his accusations, she said, 'Ask your father, he'll tell you.'

'The tale you've cooked up together, no doubt. He's besotted with you, but afraid to tell me because he knows how I feel.'

'Your father's not well,' she said quietly, striving to keep her temper in check, which was difficult in the face of his censure. 'He's spending the morning in bed. If I hadn't asked him about this I wouldn't have been able to get on with my work.'

His expression changed for one fleeting moment. 'What's wrong with him? Why didn't you fetch me?'

'It's nothing more than a headache, it wasn't worth bothering you.'

'But an excuse all the same for you to spend time in his bedroom.' His lips were grim and his eyes had never been so coldly accusing. 'If I had my way I'd throw you out of the house right now!'

'Then it's a good job Charles employed me and not you!' she cried, turning away from him in disgust and heading for the stairs.

He followed. 'I've not finished with you yet.' His fingers dug into her shoulders, effectively stopping her retreat. 'I want your

158

word that you'll lay off pestering him. He has enough on his plate with Zelah without you adding to his troubles.'

Fuming beneath her breath, Corrie swung round, her blue eyes blazing. 'How dare you insinuate such a thing! I tell you, Charles is ill. That's the only reason I was in his room. Check for yourself if you don't believe me.'

The sound of an opening door made them both turn and look back along the landing. Charles, fully dressed, and looking as fit as ever, came out. 'What's going on? Why are you two arguing?'

There was silence for a few minutes. Corrie was surprised that he had got ready so quickly, but relieved that he was now here to convince his son that he spoke nonsense. 'Charles!' She moved towards him, holding out her hand. 'You shouldn't have got up, but now you're here please tell Damon that it's all nonsense, that—'

She got no further. Damon had disappeared, but not before she had had time to see the look of loathing on his face.

Charles caught her hand, clearly puzzled. 'Corrie, my child, what's all this about? What's wrong with Damon?'

She shook her head sadly, trying to banish the hurt that had cut through her like a knife. 'It's not important, not any more.'

And Charles, with his acute sense of perception, did not pursue the matter.

The rest of the day passed much the same as any other one and Corrie thought she had succeeded in pushing the unpleasant scene with Damon to the back of her mind. It was not until much later, when she was alone in her room before dinner, that it all came tumbling back.

It was the look on Damon's face that upset her. If ever a man had hated her it was him. There seemed little chance now of anything ever developing between them. His opinion of her was all too clear. His father's appearance had been the final conclusive evidence that he needed. He was hopelessly wrong, but she knew that no amount of argument on her part would alter his opinion. He had made up his mind from the beginning and that was that.

She washed and changed into her striped dress, not really interested in her appearance, not even noting that her face looked wan and there were dark shadows beneath her eyes.

It came as a surprise when Damon was present for dinner. It had been so long now since he joined them that she knew that their earlier argument must have something to do with it. More surprising still was the fact that he asked her to go out for a ride with him.

'Why?' she asked, disregarding Charles'

curious stare at her abrupt question.

'I think you know the reason,' replied Damon succinctly, 'without me going into details.'

'But I don't,' interjected his father. 'Nor do I know why you were arguing earlier. Would someone mind telling me what's going on?'

'My quarrel is with Corrie,' said Damon. 'There are a few things I wish to discuss with her—in private.'

But the older man was more astute than his son thought. 'If it concerns me then I have a right to be present.'

Damon looked steadily at his father. 'Where did you get that idea from?'

'Putting two and two together,' returned Charles evenly. 'It wasn't difficult.'

Damon's suspicious eyes travelled across to Corrie. 'Was it you? Did you go running to him, crying on his shoulder that his big bad son had been shouting at you, accusing you of not playing the game?'

Inside Corrie cried. How much more cruel could he get? Had he no idea what his taunts did to her? But rather than let either of the Courtneys know how she felt she tilted her chin defiantly. 'I'm not a baby, Damon, I can stand on my own two feet. Say and think what you like, it makes no difference.' She only hoped he would believe her. It would be humiliating beyond belief for him to guess how deep his remarks cut.

'I think your behaviour towards Corrie is intolerable,' said Charles. 'I can't understand you, Damon. What have you got against the child?'

'Against Corrie herself—nothing. Against her attitude—everything.' Damon spoke harshly, unsympathetically. 'You amaze me, Father. You're so blind. If I don't do something heaven knows what sort of a mess you'll get yourself into!'

Charles pushed himself up from the table impatiently. 'You're barking up the wrong tree, son. I love Corrie, but it's purely paternal. Can't you see that? I'm not such a fool as you make out.'

'And Corrie, how does she regard you?' spat Damon viciously. 'In the same light? I hardly think so. I know what I've seen between you two and if this is some cock and bull story designed to fob me off you can both think again!'

Corrie looked at Charles, wondering how he would take these explosive comments, and was surprised when he walked out of the room. Perhaps he didn't want a showdown in front of her, maybe he would tackle his son later. She did not know, but all her sympathies lay with Charles and she really hated Damon for what he was doing to him.

'How could you?' she cried heatedly. 'Your own father, how can you treat him like this? Doesn't he mean anything to you? Can't you see you've hurt him?'

'You think I'm not hurt?' he replied. 'You think this affair means nothing to me?' His eyes were shadowed and angry, his mouth hard and taut. 'I'm sick of it. I wish to God I'd never brought you here. I ought to have known you would bring nothing but trouble!'

For a moment Corrie felt compassion, but only briefly. This man did not deserve pity, he was heartless and cruel and could see no other side of an argument except his own.

'You bring trouble on yourself,' she said rashly, 'with your stupid insistence that I'm like Zelah. Can't you see any further than the end of your nose? Perhaps it might be a good idea if we met, then you would see for yourself what the difference is.'

He said calmly, 'I prefer to rely on my own judgment.'

'Or your memory,' she returned, eyes blazing passionately. 'I think perhaps you've allowed time to colour it. You remember only the bad things about Zelah. I'm quite sure there must have been some good in her, otherwise Charles would never have made her his wife.'

Damon laughed drily. 'She could be charming when she wanted, I won't argue with that. It's her ability to devour men that sticks in my throat.'

Corrie eyed him haughtily. 'I can't claim the same fault.'

'Perhaps you don't know yourself,' came the bland reply. 'Tramps like you act unconsciously, it's in their blood.'

Fighting back furious tears, Corrie said, 'Have I made a pass at you? If it's true, what you say, surely you'd be the obvious target? Young, handsome, virile, rich into the bargain. Perfect in every sense for a woman who's out for all she can get.'

Their eyes met and held for several long seconds. Corrie was the first to look away, her heart pounding. Even in the midst of this argument he still held the power to attract her, to fill her with a wanton desire that was almost too great to bear.

'I've no doubt,' he said coldly, 'that had I given you the slightest encouragement you'd be all over me now, as you are my father.'

Ignoring this latter thrust, Corrie returned bitingly, 'You think I'd be attracted to *you*? How conceited can you get! Why, you're the most insolent, despicable, infuriating man I've ever met!'

His eyes widened. 'Are you saying that you

would be able to resist me? That you could coolly shrug aside my advances and declare they mean nothing to you? Try again, little Corrie. I know you better than that.'

She glared. 'You don't know me at all. You only think you do.'

'Am I supposed to take it from that that my kisses leave you cold?' He sounded amused. 'If that's the case I'd like to see you when someone turns you on. Perhaps I might try it. I wonder what would happen if I really tried to break down your defences. Would you be as immune to me as you make out?'

The conversation was becoming uncomfortable. Corrie slid out of her chair, her meal still untouched.

'Where are you going?' he asked abruptly.

She said stiffly, 'Is it any business of yours?'

'I think it is. Was the conversation not to your liking? Are you perhaps going to seek comfort with my father?' He too stood up and barred her exit from the kitchen. 'The ride's still on. We'll leave this lot and go now. You won't need a coat, the night's warm, but should you feel cold my car has an excellent heater.'

Gripping her arm, he led her forcibly from the room. Even then his touch evoked a burning desire and she wanted to swing round into his arms and beg him to understand. The

165

knowledge that such a plea would prove futile was all that stopped her.

The Rolls was waiting, indicating that he had planned this trip beforehand. He pushed her unceremoniously inside before sliding into the driver's seat and nosing the big car out of the yard.

Corrie looked steadfastly out of the window, trying to ignore the man at her side. To begin with the road was narrow, switchbacking between rows of thorn trees which appeared to be reaching up to seek air. Next they drove through a silken green tunnel where the light filtered in through the tracery of leaves.

A flock of sheep appeared as if from nowhere and they found themselves surrounded by baaing fleeces. Soon they were out in the open and Damon put down his foot. Granite boulders sparkled in the evening sun, tree-covered slopes climbed away from them. Verdant and peaceful, it made Corrie almost forget her troubles.

Occasionally they passed an Irish traveller trudging along in his sackcloth clothes, very often lifting his hand in salute, his none too clean weatherbeaten face breaking into a gap-toothed smile.

'Where do they sleep?' asked Corrie, her curiosity getting the better of her as she looked back along the road to watch the bent figure disappear from view.

'Anywhere,' shrugged Damon. 'A bed of straw somewhere, even on the roadside.'

'And what do they eat?'

'Whatever they can scrounge. They cook it over a fire of green faggots and if you get close enough you can smell the smoke in their clothes. They rarely wash, yet they're remarkably healthy. They seem to enjoy their chosen life style.'

Corrie wrinkled her nose. 'It wouldn't suit me.'

'Everyone's entitled to choose the way they live.'

There was something in the way he spoke that made Corrie think he was indirectly referring to Zelah—and herself—and she looked at him quickly ready to make a sharp rejoinder, but his face was expressionless as he looked ahead at the road unfolding before them. 'I'll take you to Waterford one of these days to see the superb glass they make there,' he said matter-of-factly.

'I'd like that,' she replied simply. 'My mother—Anne—has a Waterford crystal vase that I've always admired.'

'Maybe I'll buy you one,' he said with an oblique smile, 'for your bottom drawer.'

'There won't be any need for that,' she said

tautly. 'I've sent my letter to John. The engagement's off.'

'So you're a free agent?'

Corrie lifted her slim shoulders and grimaced prettily. 'You could put it like that.'

'Then there's nothing to stop me—making a pass at you?'

The question was surprising. She said, 'I didn't notice it stopping you before.'

'Ah, but I held back,' he replied with considerable amusement. 'I knew I was trespassing on another man's property.'

'I think you're sending me up,' she said crossly, 'and I don't find it very funny.'

Almost before she was aware of his intentions the car slid smoothly to a halt at the side of the road and Damon's arm was across her shoulders, pulling her inexorably towards him.

Her eyes shot open in surprise and she struggled desperately. 'What game are you playing?'

'I'm proving that it was no joke,' he drawled, one firm hand lifting her chin. 'You're very attractive. You have an untouched look about you, surprising I suppose under the circumstances.' His finger touched her lips as she opened her mouth to protest. 'But it makes you infinitely appealing. So many times I've wanted to kiss you, but—'

'You've remembered my status with John,' she finished disbelievingly. 'Try pulling the other one! What you mean is that you've had the inclinations but you've endeavoured to keep them in check because of what you think I am—not because of any code of ethics.'

'We won't argue the point now,' he said, his mouth drawing close. When she tried to pull away his other hand came round to hold her against him.

'I demand that you let me go!' she cried.

'When I'm good and ready,' came the insolent reply, his warm breath fanning her cheek.

When his lips travelled down the curve of her throat to the soft pulse which beat furiously at its base Corrie felt exquisite tingles of desire race through her; white-hot excitement and an indescribable urge to respond, but she knew that to do so would be fatal. Somehow she had to show Damon that his attentions meant nothing, convince him that she and Zelah were poles apart.

Somewhere she heard frenzied heartbeats—her own mingling with his, both pulsing at twice their normal rate. It would be difficult to stem the urgency which flowed through him now. It truly felt as though he had thrown caution to the winds and was determined to

169

take whatever she might offer with no thought whether he was doing right or wrong.

When his mouth claimed hers in a hard ruthless kiss she felt herself being carried away like a petal in a storm, tossed and buffeted until she did not know which way she was going. She heard herself groan weakly and he pursued her hungrily, relentlessly, his hand sensuously caressing her skin beneath the dress he had unbuttoned in his eagerness.

She could not deny her need of him, or the fact that his expertise awoke a longing she had never known existed, but through sheer determination she stopped her lips from responding. Fire there was inside her, but outwardly she maintained a cool she was far from feeling, lying impassive in his arms, her only betrayal that soft moan which had escaped before she was aware of it.

Not until he had satisfied his own need of her did Damon stop, and then she clung to him dizzily, reluctant to admit that although she had striven desperately to hide her rampant feelings he must be aware of her inner torment, might even now be gloating about the power he held over her.

An assumption confirmed a few moments later when he said, 'An admirable attempt, my dear lady, but not convincing enough.'

'For what?' she snapped, her eyes bright

with temper. 'To convince a maniac like you that I'm impassive? I've never tried to deny it.'

A smile curved his wide lips, his handsome face still hovering dangerously close. 'It must be a change for you, to play a retiring part instead of the *femme fatale*.'

'Just as it's a change for you to chase me after your avowal of hatred for my sex,' she said coldly. 'Perhaps it's me who ought to be asking you whether you're feeling frustrated.'

'It's different for a man,' he said lightly. 'Any girl is willing to give him what he wants. I think I can safely say I wasn't kissing you because I wanted satisfaction.'

Her glance held scorn. '*Any* girl? You ought to get your facts right before making rash statements like that.'

He lifted his brows coolly. 'I mean what I say. With the right approach any girl can be won over.'

Corrie shook her head in furious agitation. 'I don't see the point in this conversation, it's getting us nowhere. Please take me home.'

'In due course,' he said with a satisfied smile. 'I've not finished with you yet.'

She flushed and then went pale. 'What more do you want, for goodness' sake, haven't you humiliated me enough?'

'That was not my intention,' he said calmly.

'I've decided it's time we were friends. I've not succeeded in getting rid of you—so I see no point in further hostilities.'

Corrie's mouth fell open as she looked at him, her blue eyes incredulous. 'I don't believe you. There must be some ulterior motive behind it.' She wanted to believe him, desperately, but how could she?

'Why should there be?' he asked innocently.

'Because up till now you've made no secret of the fact that you can't stand the sight of me.'

'Correction, I never said that. On the contrary, I have always found you extremely desirable.' He lifted his hand to touch her cheek, but she slapped it away angrily. 'And,' he continued imperturbably, 'I think the time has come to remedy the rift between us.'

She could not help but feel excited at the thought of being friends with Damon, perhaps more than that, lovers even. It caused her heartbeats to accelerate once more and a warm glow colour her cheeks. But what she really wanted to know was the reason behind his offer. Without sincerity it could mean nothing and she could see no possible cause for him to alter his opinion.

But when his lips once more brushed hers all sane thoughts departed. She closed her

172

eyes and revelled in this unexpected pleasure. Time later to puzzle over his sudden change of heart.

CHAPTER NINE

The pattern of Corrie's life changed after that. Damon paid her more attention than ever before and most evenings they went out together, sometimes for a ride, occasionally for a meal.

He even intruded on the hours she spent working on Charles' book, and she wondered why he was not giving so much time to his farming as formerly. One thought that kept thrusting itself to the foreground but which she persistently pushed away was that he had set himself up as a watchdog. The whole thing was planned to keep her away from Charles as much as possible. It had to be the truth. She could think of no other reason why Damon should suddenly pay her so much attention. It was nice, admittedly, and she infinitely preferred it to the enmity he had shown earlier, but it somewhat spoiled the pleasure of his friendship.

Each time she was out with him she could not help but feel it was all a game he was playing. He could not be jealous, for she knew without a shadow of doubt that he was not attracted towards her. It had to be because he was afraid his father would make a fool of himself over her. Stupid really, there was no possible chance of that happening, but Damon had it firmly fixed in his mind that there was something going on between them and this was his way of putting a stop to it.

One night, when this thought was bothering Corrie more than usual, she taxed him with it. They had driven into Dublin for a meal and then gone on to a dance hall. Damon's arms were about her as they drifted round the floor to a dreamy waltz. To all outward appearances they were lovers engrossed only in each other. Corrie's head was resting on Damon's broad shoulder, his arms held her close and she ought to have been deliriously happy. Instead she felt uneasy and wriggled restlessly against him. 'Let's sit down,' she said. 'I suddenly don't feel like dancing.'

'As you like,' came the bland reply, and he led her back towards their seats. 'Is something the matter, you look worried?'

'I want to know why you're bothering with me,' she burst out bitterly, her pent-up emotions of the last few days at last overflowing.

His dark eyes sparkled. 'I'm taking advantage of the situation. I'd be insane not to enjoy the company of a pretty girl like you while you're a guest in our house.'

'I don't believe you,' she said bluntly, drawing in a deep breath before continuing, 'I think it's because of Charles. You're trying to keep me away from him.' She looked expectantly across at Damon, wishing she could ignore the weakness caused by his close proximity.

A frown narrowed his eyes. 'Is that an admission that you're missing him, that you would prefer his company to mine?'

'It's nothing of the sort,' she countered hotly.

'It's a damn insult,' he said savagely. 'Is my company so intolerable that you prefer that of a man three times your age?'

Corrie sighed in exasperation. 'I've told you that that's not the reason. I'm only here to help him with his book, nothing more.'

'In that case,' he said with ill-concealed impatience, 'it can't matter that your own time is spent with me.'

'It's not that I mind being with you. I like your company,' she said hastily. 'But it's why that bothers me.'

'Why should it?' he asked coolly. 'I can't imagine the reasons behind a man asking you out have ever bothered you before.'

Corrie tossed her head in anger. 'The circumstances are slightly different. In the beginning you made no attempt to hide your dislike of me. Why the sudden change?'

Damon grinned. 'I don't think it necessary for you to worry your pretty head about the whys and wherefores of our relationship. Sufficient for the moment to take what's offered, don't you think?'

'If you're offering yourself to me,' she flung angrily, 'you can forget it. You're not my type.'

His smile still lingered. 'Ah, I forgot, it's the estimable John who took your fancy, or am I wrong? Is it perhaps the older man, someone with plenty of money, a sucker for a beautiful girl?'

Had they not been in public Corrie would have slapped him across the face. Instead she had to content herself with saying hotly, 'You're insane! You've a twisted mind, and I ought to have known better than to ask.'

'So you had,' he said pleasantly. 'Am I to take it that this conversation is at an end? If so, I suggest we resume our dance.'

Corrie glared. 'I don't want you to touch me again. I don't like what you're doing.'

His face hardened. 'And I don't like what you're insinuating. Perhaps you're right, it is

176

time we went.' He scraped back his chair and stood up, waiting until Corrie had picked up her handbag before leading the way back to his car.

She said nothing until they were in the Rolls and on their way, but her anger had not abated and she turned to him, only just able to make out the bare outline of his face in the light from the dashboard. 'I hope this has put an end to the farcical situation you've created.'

'Not in the least.' His tone was grim and she was aware of the tension inside him. 'I shall continue to take you out whenever I feel like it.'

'And if I refuse?'

'You will not be allowed to say no,' he returned decisively.

Corrie fumed. 'If you think you're going to boss over me you're mistaken. I do what I want.'

'And *I* do what *I* want,' he said, 'so it looks as though it's going to be a question of who's the stronger.' For the first time his lips relented. 'I wonder who'll win.'

She refused to answer and stared stormily ahead at the channel of light made by their headlights, wondering why on earth she had had to fall in love with such an impossible man. It looked as though the brief period of respite was over and she could blame no one

177

but herself. If she had not attempted to find out what motivated his actions there could still have been that rapport between them that had become infinitely dear to her. Now it would more than likely revert to rows all the time.

It was still comparatively early when they arrived home and there was a car parked in front of the house. Corrie assumed it was a visitor for either Damon or Charles and decided to go straight to bed. She did not feel that she could put on a false front for the benefit of strangers, not tonight when her world was slowly falling to pieces.

But she had been in her room for no more than a few seconds when the door opened and Damon came in. 'What do you want?' she asked snappily, fearing he might have it in mind to continue their argument.

'Your boy-friend's arrived.' His face was expressionless, telling her nothing about his reaction to John's presence. 'Just as I said— he's entirely predictable.'

Corrie's first reaction was one of dismay. She had not wanted John here, that was why she had sent the letter. But after a few moments she realised that this could be the answer to her problems. Damon would no longer worry that she might seek Charles' company and consequently would leave her alone.

'Tell him I'll be down in a minute,' she said, and waited for him to go. 'I'd like to comb my hair.' In reality she did not want to go downstairs with Damon, she preferred to meet John alone. They had much to discuss and she knew for a fact that he would not be in a very good humour.

'You surprise me,' said Damon. 'I thought you'd rush down no matter what you look like.'

'You forget,' she said coolly, 'our engagement's over.'

'On your part maybe, but the boy-friend looks very determined. I think you'd better prepare yourself.' He moved towards the door, adding as he let himself out, 'From one battle to another. I wonder who'll be the victor out of you two.'

Childishly Corrie bobbed out her tongue as he closed the door, but forgot his taunt a few moments later as she too left the room ready for her confrontation with John.

He was in the sitting room, perched on the edge of the gold settee looking distinctly uncomfortable. Damon stood with his back to the fireplace, although there was no fire burning, and Charles occupied one of the armchairs.

'Ah, Corrie, my dear,' said the older man. 'I've been keeping your young man entertained. A pity you were out when he came, but never mind, we'll leave you two together now. I expect you have a lot to talk about.'

With that he and his son left the room, but not before Damon had given her a look which seemed to suggest that the battle was on.

As the door closed John stood up and came across to Corrie, who still stood hesitantly just inside the room. He stood rigidly before her, his brown eyes hurt and an expression on his face such as she had never seen before—sad yet defensive, as though he was trying to hold back a torrent of angry words. 'Perhaps you'd better tell me what this is all about,' he said tightly.

Corrie nodded and bit her lip nervously. 'Shall we sit down? There's so much happened I don't really know where to begin.'

He resumed his seat on the settee and she sat beside him, her fingers twisting in her lap.

John spoke first. 'I don't like deceit, Corrie, I'd never have thought you capable of it. Why?'

'Why what?' she asked, stalling him, yet knowing full well that he referred to Damon. Not once had she mentioned him in her letters, preferring him to believe that she lived only with Charles Courtney.

'You know,' he said bluntly. 'This guy

180

Damon—who is he, and why haven't you mentioned him? Is there something going on between you? Is that the reason you want to break off our engagement?'

Corrie replied hastily, 'Of course not. He means nothing to me. I'm working for his father, that's all. I did tell you that.'

'It's what you didn't tell me that's the issue. Are you in love with him?'

'Heavens, no!' she cried quickly, too quickly perhaps for John looked unconvinced. 'We hate each other.'

'Then why were you out dancing with him? Sounds funny to me.'

Corrie shrugged. 'Why shouldn't I? You don't have to be in love with a person to go out with him.'

'You at least have to like him,' he said coldly. 'There's more to this than you're admitting—and I mean to find out.'

'John,' Corrie touched his knee. 'Please—don't probe. Take my word for it that we have nothing going for each other.'

He picked up her hand and held it close between his own. 'I'd like to, Corrie, really I would, but I can only believe the evidence before my eyes. When I knew you were working for Charles Courtney I didn't like it, not living in the same house. But if I'd known there were two of them—and particularly that

181

damned handsome devil who's been eyeing me as though I'm like something he's never seen before—well, I ask you, what do you expect me to feel? I'm telling you, Corrie, if I'd known the true circumstances I'd have been over here long ago. It was very wrong of you to try and deceive me.'

Corrie said, 'I'm sorry, John,' and hoped she looked suitably penitent. 'I shouldn't have done it, but I knew how you'd feel, and really, there's nothing at all for you to get het up about.'

He dropped her hand and stood up. 'Nothing? How can you say that? We were going to get married when you came back from this tomfool trip. I knew I should never have let you come alone—I suppose I'm to blame for the whole darn thing.'

'No, you're not, John,' Corrie said softly. 'Perhaps I never really loved you and it took this break to make me realise it. It's better that I should find out now than after we're married, don't you think?'

He shook his head savagely. 'I still think that Damon fellow has something to do with it. What on earth made you stay here, Corrie? Have you given up your search for your mother?'

'This is the end of my search,' she said a trifle sadly. 'Sit down and I'll tell you about
182

it.'

He looked surprised but obeyed and Corrie continued, 'Zelah is married to Charles Courtney.'

'So you've met her!' he exclaimed. 'Why didn't you let us know? Anne's never liked to ask, but we presumed that you'd had no success. What's she like? Do you get on well?'

'Wait a minute, John!' Corrie stopped the flow of questions. 'It's not as simple as that. Zelah is—well, to put it kindly, not a very nice person. She's left Charles, for the moment, but she'll be back when she's good and ready. Charles loves her, surprisingly, but Damon hates the very mention of her name.'

John nodded, trying to understand. 'So that was the real reason you stayed on here, hoping to meet Zelah when she returned?'

'Not entirely,' said Corrie honestly. 'You see, I didn't tell Anne this because I didn't want to worry her, but I had my car stolen and Damon took pity on me and brought me back here. That's how it all started. It was a complete coincidence that Zelah happened to be married to Charles.'

'I think I'm beginning to understand,' John said slowly. 'The reason you don't get on with Damon is because you and Zelah look alike, is that it? And he dislikes you as much as he does her.'

Perhaps it was a relief that John knew the whole story, for Corrie suddenly felt easier and smiled for the first time since seeing him. 'That's right, so you see Damon really had nothing to do with my decision.'

'Then there's still hope for me?' He drew her close. 'Oh, Corrie, you don't know how much I've missed you! It's been hell, not knowing what's going on.'

She stiffened as he tried to kiss her and when his warm moist lips pressed against hers she pulled away. 'No, John, not here. Someone might come in.'

'So what?' he said hotly, resentfully. 'It's what they expect, especially the old man. He said he wondered what had taken me so long.'

'He doesn't know it's all over between us,' she said tiredly. 'But it is, John, I haven't changed my mind just because you're here, nor will I. I'm sorry, but that's the way it is.'

She didn't want to hurt his feelings by saying that his touch just now had meant nothing to her—and it was only in her heart that she would admit to comparing him with Damon. He was weak where Damon was strong. She could see that now. Why had she ever thought she loved him? The soft mouth and those pale brown eyes held none of the strength that bound her to Damon.

John, flushed and angry, said, 'You're not

184

giving yourself a chance, Corrie. You loved me before, you will again, once we're together. It's being apart that's done it, but I can assure you that it will never happen again. We'll do everything together, my darling, everything.'

'Oh, John!' Corrie looked at him with compassion. 'It won't work, I know it won't.'

'You haven't given it a chance,' he argued. 'Look, Charles Courtney has kindly asked me to stay on for a few days. Let's see how things go.'

Corrie sighed. 'As you wish, but I can't see it making any difference.'

'It will, I know it will,' he assured her confidently, once more pulling her into his arms, his eager lips seeking hers.

This time she let him kiss her, trying not to show that his embrace left her cold. He had been hurt enough without her adding to his present misery. It would be up to her to let him down gently during the next few days so that when the time came for his departure he would accept her decision, perhaps might even expect it.

CHAPTER TEN

As Corrie had expected, Charles would not allow her to work while John was there. He insisted that the two of them spend as much time together as possible, declaring that they had been apart for long enough. She had not the heart to tell him that things were different between them.

'How much longer do you intend staying?' she asked John on the evening of his second day. Supper was over and they were together in the sitting room. Charles made a habit of being conspicuously absent these days and of Damon they saw hardly anything. He worked hard and Corrie guessed that he was making up for lost time.

'Is that a hint that you want me gone?' he asked irritably.

John was not so passive as he used to be and she said now in an attempt to soothe him, 'Of course not, dear. I was only thinking of Charles' book. It's very kind of him to give me time off, but I can't expect him to pay me a wage while I'm enjoying myself with you.'

It was on these last words that John pounced. 'Ah, so my company's not so bad after all,' and he pulled her into his arms. 'I knew I'd win you over in the end. Darling Corrie, I'm sorry for the things I said, but I was jealous of that damned brute. Now I can see for myself that I was mistaken—and I can afford to wait. You'll see, things will soon be exactly as they were before.'

His kiss was warm and demanding, although it held none of the fire that Damon's did. Corrie felt guilty for comparing the two of them, but it was something that she did constantly these days. Now, though, she determinedly pushed the other man from her mind, concentrating on John as he tried to arouse some sort of response.

Consequently neither of them heard the door open and pulled apart guiltily when a sardonic voice said, 'Pardon me for intruding. Shall I come back at a more convenient time?'

Corrie flushed and smoothed her hair with a slightly unsteady hand. 'Don't be ridiculous! This is your house, you can come in when you like.'

And John said, 'I'm sorry, Courtney, but Corrie's so damned attractive. You know how it is.'

'Of course,' Damon assured him solemnly, and John appeared not to notice the underlying sarcasm, but Corrie did, and paled, clenching her fists angrily.

'You don't have to apologise to him, John,'

she said tightly.

Her eyes met Damon's, sparring momentarily before he moved further into the room and lowered himself on to one of the armchairs, a leg hung carelessly over the arm. 'I have some news that might interest you,' he said. 'Your car's been found, minus, needless to say, your handbag.'

'But that's wonderful!' She forgot her anger and smiled at both Damon and John. 'That's great. Where is it?'

'Not far from here,' he said shortly, 'but I shouldn't be too happy about it.'

'Why not?' she asked, puzzled.

'It's a write-off. Joy-riders apparently, kids out for a kick. Wouldn't be surprised if it wasn't some of that gang you were smooching with. It's a good trick if you can get away with it.'

'Gang?' asked John instantly. 'What's this, Corrie? You never said anything about meeting anyone else.'

'Oh, take no notice of him,' she cried heatedly. 'He's exaggerating.'

Damon lifted his brows and looked directly at John. 'Perhaps it's time you learned a few home truths about your—er—girl-friend. She's not as innocent as she looks. Twice I found her in trouble with the boys. She takes after her mother in that direction. Has she

188

told you about Zelah?'

John nodded, looking at first bemused and then angry. When he spoke his voice was harsh. 'I shall want to hear more about this, Corrie, but I'll wait until we're alone.'

Damon rose, looking well pleased with himself. 'I'll go then, leave you two lovebirds to sort it out. Sorry if I've thrown the cat among the pigeons so to speak, but I thought you ought to know, John, what's been going on behind your back.'

'I hate you,' snapped Corrie, more to herself than to him, but he heard and laughed.

'A good healthy response, just what I expected. But I've no doubt, little Corrie, that you'll be able to talk yourself out of it, just as you try to talk yourself out of every other situation. Let me know the result, I shall be interested to hear.'

The moment the door closed John rounded on her hotly. Corrie could not recall seeing him in a temper before, he was the most placid person she had ever met. Now, though, his face was red and his mouth worked angrily. 'It seems I came not a moment too soon. Would you mind telling me what's been going on?'

Corrie rose and walked a few steps away before turning to look down at him sadly. 'Don't you trust me, John? Are you really going to take the word of that pompous brute?'

'He doesn't strike me as the sort of person who would lie.'

'No,' she cut in quickly, 'but he embroiders the truth, and that's just as bad.'

John folded his arms and looked up at her. He was still angry but well in control of his feelings. 'Perhaps you would like to tell me your version and I'll make up my own mind who to believe.'

'I don't see why I should,' she said coldly. 'After all, it's all over between us, so what does it matter to you now?'

'A great deal,' he replied promptly. 'I'm not letting you go without a fight, Corrie, and if there's no other man involved—well, I reckon it won't take me long to get back on the same footing as we were before.'

She said drily, 'I'll say this for you, John Marshall, you're very determined, you surprise me. I never thought you'd turn up here, as a matter of fact, I thought my letter would be sufficient to assure you that it was all over between us. Damon was right for once.'

'Damon? What has he got to do with it? What interest has he in our private affairs?'

'He knew about the letter,' she said defensively. 'He happened to come in while I was writing it and—well, I found myself telling him about you. He said it was the one

190

thing guaranteed to make you come rushing over. I disagreed.'

'I still don't see why you discussed it with him,' charged John. 'I suspect there's more between you two than you'd have me know.'

Corrie shook her head in exasperation. 'Heavens, John, I can't stand the man! Surely that's obvious enough for any fool to see?'

John appeared thoughtful. 'Mmm, I wonder, and what's this about these other fellows you've been knocking about with? You seem to have been having a grand old time behind my back.'

Before answering Corrie moved to the armchair Damon had used only minutes earlier. She sat down, sighing deeply. 'There's nothing to it. I was trying to find out from one of the boys whether he knew Zelah. We got talking and he invited me to their beach party, that's all.'

'It's not what Damon insinuated. What time did this party go on till?'

She shrugged. 'I've no idea. I left before the end.'

'Why, because things were getting out of hand?' he asked cuttingly. 'It's what it looks like to me. I'm surprised at you, Corrie, I never thought you were a girl like that.'

'I'm not, for heaven's sake,' she insisted angrily. 'Why do men always think the

191

worst?'

'And something else,' he accused. 'You never said you'd had your car stolen. That's another lie you've lived. I'm beginning to wonder what is truth and what isn't.'

Corrie sprang to her feet. 'You can believe what you like, I've had enough of this cross-examination! If you want to know anything else ask Damon, he appears to have all the answers.'

John tried to stop her, but she shrugged off his restraining hand and dashed upstairs to her room. She sat down before the dressing table and looked at her flaming face. Her fine pale hair looked wild and her wide blue eyes sparkled angrily. 'I hate men!' she addressed her reflection. 'They're nothing but trouble—except Charles, of course.' Her face softened at the thought of Damon's father and suddenly she had the urge to talk to him. He would make her feel better. She had missed him this last couple of days.

Without even stopping to brush her hair Corrie went to find Charles. She tried his study first, risking the fact that she might bump into John again, but it was empty; so too was the kitchen. That only left his bedroom. She was a little hesitant about intruding on his privacy, but her desperate need to talk to him won.

Her knock was answered immediately. She found Charles sitting near the window reading, but he put down his book as soon as he saw who his visitor was. 'Corrie, my dear, how nice of you to come and see me! I must say John seems a nice boy—I'm glad for you, child, you could have done worse.'

Corrie sank down on to the edge of the bed, her face troubled. 'It's all over between us, Charles. That's why he came. I wrote and told him the engagement's off. The trouble is he won't take no for an answer.'

Charles looked stunned and for a moment she regretted telling him. It was hardly fair to drag him into her troubles.

'I'm sorry, Corrie,' he said. 'I didn't realise. Is that why you're here now, to discuss your problems?'

'If you don't mind—I have no one else.'

He smiled kindly. 'Fire away, child. You know I think of you as my daughter.'

'John thinks I've been up to all sorts of things and he's very angry. Damon told him about those boys—you know, that night he brought me here. Then I hadn't told him my car had been stolen. He thinks I've been shooting him a whole pack of lies. He says he doesn't know what to believe now.'

She looked so miserable that Charles came and stood by her, resting his hand lightly on her shoulders. 'You know what they say about the course of true love.'

'But I don't love him,' cried Corrie. 'I thought I did, once, but now I don't, I love—' She broke off, regretting that slip of the tongue that had almost caused her to admit her true feelings.

'I know,' said Charles slowly. 'You love my son.'

For one electrifying moment all Corrie could do was look up at Charles, her eyes wide and disbelieving. 'H-how did you know?' she managed to husk at last.

'I'm not blind,' said Charles with a smile. 'I see what goes on.'

'But is it so obvious?' she gasped. 'I mean, Damon, does he know?' The thought was shattering.

But Charles shook his head reassuringly. 'Damon has this obsession that all women are evil, I'm sorry.'

'It's not your fault,' she said passionately. 'It has nothing to do with you.'

Charles sat beside her. 'In a way it has. You see, my first wife left me too, when Damon was about fourteen. She's dead now, we never divorced, but—well, it left a scar on Damon's heart that was only just healing when I met Zelah.'

He paused a moment, reflecting on the

past, and Corrie was afraid to intrude on his thoughts. A moment later he continued, 'He's had a few girl-friends, but never anything serious. He's very wary, he trusts no-one, and it's only because of what's happened to me. Perhaps I'm unlucky, I don't know. There are plenty of good women in the world—you, for instance, my dear. I would like to see you married to Damon. It's been my biggest hope ever since you came.'

'Was that why you offered me the job?' she asked breathlessly, upset by what she had just heard, but more able to appreciate Damon's attitude.

He smiled and nodded. 'Partly, but also because I really did need someone and you fitted the bill admirably.'

She pulled his hand into her own. 'Thank you for telling me—about everything. I'm sorry things didn't go right for you, but it's all much clearer now. Do you think Damon will ever change his mind?'

Charles shrugged. 'Time alone will tell. He's a fool. He thinks me one, I know, but at least I'm aware of Zelah's shortcomings, was before I married her, but love's not something you can ignore, is it?'

And Corrie could truthfully answer him that it was not.

'But what am I going to do about John?' she

asked, tenderly stroking the back of his hand. 'I've told him I hate Damon, though I think he's even beginning to have his doubts about that.'

'You must ask yourself whether your love for my son is strong enough for you to wait, perhaps for a long, long time—years even—until he realises that you're not so bad as he thinks, or whether you're prepared to settle for second best.'

Corrie's eyes shone. 'I'd wait for ever if I thought there was even a remote chance that he might change his mind about me. Do you think there is, Charles, do you?'

Her eager question brought a smile to his lips and he raised her hand and pressed it to his mouth. 'Bless you, child, with love like that how can you go wrong? But you must tell John the truth, there's no other way out of it.'

She sighed and nodded slowly. 'I suppose so—but it won't be easy. He'll know then that I've been lying all along.'

'So what,' said Charles. 'Does it really matter now? You can't keep him dangling, that's for sure, so a clean break is by far the best way. And I insist that you write and tell your—parents. They at least are entitled to the truth.'

'I will.' She pushed herself up, her face thoughtful. 'I'll do it tomorrow.'

Her talk with Charles had done her good and she felt much happier now than she had a half hour earlier. He really was a dear and she was grateful to him for explaining the reason behind Damon's hostile behaviour. It made things so much more clear that she was even smiling as she let herself out of the room.

But her smile faded when she practically bumped into Damon who appeared also to be about to visit his father. 'Been up to your tricks again?' he accused harshly. 'Isn't one man sufficient?'

Whatever sympathy she had felt for him vanished abruptly in the face of this accusation. 'You've a perverted mind, Damon, why don't you try asking your father what we do together?'

'I prefer to rely on what my own eyes tell me,' he said. 'You came out of my father's room looking the happiest I've seen you since John arrived. Poor John, perhaps I ought to tell him what's going on.'

'You can please yourself,' she stormed. 'It doesn't matter any more.'

She turned away, her cheeks flaming at his unspoken insinuation. But he jerked her arm back and compelled her to face him. 'Why doesn't it matter?' he snapped. 'Has he been given his marching orders?'

'Any time now,' she said distantly,

wrenching her wrist free and staring up at him defiantly. 'It's what you expected, isn't it, or did you think that once he was here he'd be able to win me back again?'

His eyes hardened. 'Any man would be a fool to marry you. Any man would be a fool to get married.'

'Just because you don't want to,' she blazed, 'it doesn't mean that it's not a good thing.'

'I've seen no good in it,' he said tightly. 'I've seen enough disaster to last me a lifetime—and all through people like you.'

It was difficult to make excuses for him when his accusations were so cruel, but Corrie knew that she must. This hard exterior he projected was a cover to hide the hurt inside. He was afraid to relax and learn to trust. Somehow she had to make him believe that not all people were as disloyal as he thought.

She said softly, 'Do you think you're being fair, blaming me for the weakness of others? We're all different, no two people are alike; can't you see that?'

'You and Zelah are, unfortunately.'

She wondered why he had tacked on that last word and a tiny ray of hope sprang to life inside her. Did it mean that deep down inside he did like her, and that it was only her remarkable resemblance to her mother that

198

made him distrust her? She smiled. 'A surface likeness, nothing more. Our natures are entirely different, Charles will tell you that.'

'I've no doubt he will,' came the cynical reply. 'I expect my father can tell me a great deal about you—but I don't like my information second hand, I prefer to find out for myself.'

'Oh, you're so stubborn!' she cried.

He looked at her with sardonic amusement. 'Docs it matter to you what I think? Are you hurt that you've met a man who hasn't fallen for your obvious charms? I shouldn't let it worry you, I know perfectly well that you get your satisfaction elsewhere.'

Corrie swung her arm round, but he was quicker than she, sidestepping neatly and grinning in an infuriating way. 'Too near the mark, was I, for your peace of mind? Perhaps you ought to be more discreet in your—er— affairs.' Without waiting for her reaction he opened his father's door and disappeared. It was surprising, thought Corrie, that Charles had not come out to see what was going on.

Damon had said some unforgivable things and she was smarting with hurt pride as she made her way back downstairs. It was no good going to bed, sleep was the farthest thing from her mind at this precise moment. She needed to escape, to go somewhere where she could forget the unpleasantness of the last few minutes.

Outside the house thoughts of the lake drew her. There it would be peaceful and calm and maybe she would be able to forget the cruel implications Damon had made. Why he should ever think that she and Charles were lovers was beyond her. Surely he had only to see the two of them together to realise that the bond between them was nothing more than a father/daughter relationship?

She reached the lake and sat down for a moment on its grassy bank. The sky was almost black, night had fallen quickly and she had only the pendulous silvery moon and a handful of stars for company.

Unbidden came thoughts of the last time she had been here with Damon. It was the closest she had come to making a fool of herself. His kisses had evoked responses she had never before dreamed about and if he hadn't pushed her away goodness knows what might have happened.

'Why do I love you, Damon?' she asked, her words sounding strangely loud in the still night air. 'Why did I have to fall for a man like you?'

A figure emerged from the shadows and Corrie's heart skitted with fright for a few seconds before she realised who it was. Even then, when she knew it was John, she wished him anywhere but here. She wanted to be alone, completely alone with her thoughts.

'So it is true,' he said stiffly as he lowered himself at her side.

Corrie's vain hope that he had not heard her cry from the heart was dashed, but at least it had made the problem of telling him easier. 'I'm afraid so,' she said, even managing to sound sad, 'not that it will do me much good. His opinion of me is as low as it can possibly be.'

'I wish you'd told me,' he said plaintively. 'You've made me a right laughing stock.'

Corrie shook her head. 'No, I haven't. Damon doesn't know how I feel. I expect he thinks there's still a chance that we might patch things up.'

'And will we?' he asked eagerly. 'I mean, if he doesn't return your love then there's not much point in hankering after him.'

'It's a chance I must take,' she said softly but firmly. 'I'm sorry, John, I was going to tell you in the morning. If I can't have Damon I'd rather never marry than make you an unsatisfactory wife.'

'But that might not be the case,' he argued. 'We were happy before you came to Ireland, why not again? Given time you'll push him out of your mind. I'll be patient, really I will.'

Knowing how futile her own future was Corrie was tempted to agree, but she knew deep down it would never work. Memory of Damon would fade, admittedly, but even so he would always be there at the back of her mind. She would wonder whether his attitude had changed, whether there would have been hope for her had she remained. Her job with Charles could last twelve months or more, time enough for Damon to come to terms with the truth that she was not the tramp he thought her. She had to stay to find out. There was no other answer.

'I'm sorry, John,' she whispered, 'it won't work, I know it won't. I love Damon so deeply it's unbearable. Can you understand that?'

'You never loved me like that,' he said, looking sad. 'You're right, it wouldn't work, but I wish I was the lucky man, I really do.'

She snuggled up to him, wishing she did not feel so cruel. 'Thank you for understanding, and if I've hurt you, I'm sorry.'

His arm encircled her shoulders. 'Just remember, Corrie, if you ever need me, I'll be there. Like you, I shall never love anyone else. I wish you luck.'

Tears welled in Corrie's eyes, spilling over and rolling down her cheeks. John was a fine man, he did not deserve what she was doing to him.

'Hey, what's this?' he asked, observing her tears and tilting her chin so that he could look into her face. 'Not for me, surely?'

She nodded. 'I feel awful—you're so good and kind, and look what I'm doing.'

'It's life,' he said resignedly. 'You can't win every time. Do you want me to go back home straight away, or would you like me to stay and hold your hand for a while? He can be pretty damning, that man of yours.'

'Would you?' she appealed worriedly. 'It wouldn't be asking too much, I shall understand if you want to go, but it would be nice to have you here.'

'I'm made of sterner stuff than you,' he smiled, squeezing her gently. 'I'll stay for a couple of days anyway. I've some holiday due, so no one's going to quibble.'

He had taken the whole thing much better than Corrie had expected. The trouble was it made her feel worse than ever, him being so nice about it.

They stayed out for another hour, sometimes talking, sometimes sitting quietly, looking out across the still waters. There was something comforting about John now. He would act as a buffer between her and Damon, and for this she was grateful.

203

When they eventually arrived back at the house Damon was in the hall. His dark eyes glittered as he looked Corrie insolently up and down. 'Two in one day—you're lucky.'

Aware that John was about to say something in her defence Corrie tugged his arm, saying, 'Don't waste your breath. It's his only pleasure, trying to see how cruel he can be to me. I don't take any notice, not any more. He's not worth it.'

But even as she spoke tears glistened in her eyes and she was thankful for John leading her away. They went upstairs together and, although she did not look back, she knew that Damon watched, and condemned. It was enough to break her heart altogether and she began to doubt the wisdom of her decision to stay.

'Keep a stiff upper lip,' whispered John in her ear. 'Remember, you're going to win in the end.'

CHAPTER ELEVEN

As soon as she woke the next morning Corrie duly wrote her letter to Anne and David telling them that her engagement to John was off, but that they remained good friends and that he was staying on for a few more days.

She still made no mention of Damon—it was not something she could put into words. To state baldly that she had fallen in love with another man, but that he did not love her, would send Anne into a tizzy. Anne was very fond of John and would certainly be distressed by this news, with the further worry that Corrie was wasting her life loving some man who did not even return her feelings.

Over breakfast she said to John, 'Do you think you could find something to do if I carry on with Charles' book today? Apart from feeling guilty at letting him down, the work will help take my mind off—other things.'

John nodded, understanding perfectly. 'Go ahead. I'll take myself off on a long walk and explore the countryside.'

Corrie knew he would enjoy that. Walking had always been one of their favourite pastimes. 'I'll cut you some sandwiches,' she said. 'I almost wish I was coming with you— Ireland has so much to offer, don't you think, with its emerald green valleys and its towering mountains? I've really fallen in love with it.'

'I can see that,' he said softly. 'I've lost you to both the man and the country. What Anne and David will say if you decide to settle down here I don't know. They'll be very upset.'

Corrie nodded sadly. 'I know. I've written

this morning, telling them about you and me. I didn't mention Damon, though, I couldn't. Will you tell them, when you get back?'

'Unless you come back with me,' he joked. 'I've not entirely given up hope.'

Charles came in at that moment, which fortunately gave Corrie an excuse not to answer. He greeted them cheerfully, looking from one to the other in a way that told Corrie he was wondering whether she had yet spoken to him.

'Yes, Charles,' she said, 'I've told John. It's all sorted out, but he's going to stay on a bit longer, if you don't mind?'

'Not at all,' said Charles immediately. 'Stay as long as you like, my boy. It's nice to have company. Do you play chess?'

Corrie laughed. Charles' obsession for the game amused her.

'I'm afraid I don't,' said John, looking at Corrie, wondering what was so funny. 'But I'm willing to learn.'

'That's the spirit,' said Charles. 'You can have your first lesson tonight. Damon tried to teach Corrie, but he had no luck. I guess her mind wasn't on the game.'

The twinkle in his eye told her what was in his mind and she smiled back. 'Now you're not being fair! Anyway, I've some good news for you, I'm coming back to work today. John

206

is taking himself off on a nice long walk.'

'If you're sure that's what you both want I'm delighted,' beamed Charles. 'I can't wait to get going again.'

Although Corrie had hoped that typing would take her mind off Damon she was mistaken, and when for the third time she typed Damon instead of David she tore the paper from her machine and screwing it up into a ball threw it viciously into the waste paper basket.

Charles looked round from his desk, mildly surprised at this unusual outburst from Corrie. 'What's the matter, things not going right?'

'My fingers have minds of their own today. Three times I've changed your great-grandfather's name to Damon.'

'Does he bother you so much?' asked Charles softly. 'I wish I could do something to help, but it's no good me interfering. He'd soon tell me to mind my own business.'

'I know,' she sympathised. 'I'm beginning to wonder whether it's worth it, whether I ought to forget all about him and go back to England.'

'It wouldn't do you any good,' said Charles. 'I know I'm a lot older than you, but I still know what love is all about, and my advice to you is to stick it out. If there was no hope at all, then I'd tell you, but my belief is that sooner or later Damon will realise what a wonderful person you are. Do you love him enough to wait?'

Corrie nodded. 'You know I do.'

'So why the despondency? Keep a smile on your face and go in fighting. I know I'm a fine one to talk, having had two unsuccessful marriages, but I sincerely believe that you and Damon are made for each other. I wish for nothing more than you as my daughter-in-law.'

She smiled warmly. 'I don't know what I'd do without you. With you and John behind me—he's agreed to stay on to see me through for a while, isn't that marvellous?—I shan't have time to be unhappy. I am grateful, Charles, you don't know how much.'

'Tch, tch, child, I don't want your thanks, I want your happiness. See if you can get on with your typing now. It will soon be time for lunch and you've hardly done anything.'

'Do I consider myself told off?' she laughed, turning back to her machine and inserting a fresh sheet of paper.

The day passed quickly after that. Although Damon was never far from her thoughts she was able to ignore him sufficiently to do her work with a reasonable degree of accuracy.

She was surprised when John had not

returned home in time for dinner, but not unduly worried. Unfortunately it turned out to be one of the rare occasions when Damon put in an appearance. Lately he had taken to eating at different times, but tonight, for some reason only known to himself, he joined them.

'What's happened to the boy-friend?' he asked when the three of them were seated.

Corrie's chin firmed. 'He's gone for a walk. I expect he's forgotten the time.'

'Without you?' Damon's voice held exactly the right amount of sarcasm to arouse her.

'That's right,' she said coolly. 'We don't have to do everything together. Besides, I've been getting on with your father's book.'

His eyes hardened. 'Sharing yourself between the two of them—how noble!'

'I think that's enough,' said Charles quietly. 'Why do you have to be so nasty all the time? What has Corrie done to you to make you feel this way?'

'To me? Nothing,' said Damon easily. 'It's what she's doing to you that bothers me. Are you blind, Father? Why don't you send her and that John fellow back to England where they belong? Life was so much simpler before she came along.'

'It was you who brought me here,' protested Corrie loudly. 'Why don't you try taking some of the blame?'

'It was foolish of me,' he said. 'I admit that now. But we can't put back the clock, so the only alternative is to get rid of you—the sooner the better as far as I'm concerned.'

'But that won't suit me,' said Charles. 'Corrie can stay as long as she likes, with my complete approval. I'm afraid, Damon, this is one occasion when you will not get your own way.'

Damon frowned angrily. 'I'll have a word with you later, Father.'

'It won't do any good,' replied Charles. 'You tried it before, remember? But it might do us good to bring a few things out into the open. I'll see you in my study after dinner, now I suggest we change the subject. Poor Corrie must be feeling mighty uncomfortable.'

She smiled at the older man, trying to pretend that he really had no need to feel concerned on her behalf, and not a little apprehensive about what he might be going to say to his son. She had the sneaking feeling that he might tell him about the way she felt. If possible she must have a word with him in private before he spoke to Damon. It would be too embarrassing by far to have her cause pleased for her.

But when their meal was over the two men disappeared almost before she realised it, and

Corrie was left with the clearing up and the most enormous feeling that her fate was being discussed. She did not like it, not one little bit, and this time she could not hear what was going on as all the doors were firmly closed.

When the telephone rang she half expected it to be John calling to tell them that he had forgotten the time and to apologise for missing dinner. But the voice at the other end was certainly not John's.

A man with a soft Irish brogue asked for her personally, and when she confirmed that she was Corrie Maitland he told her that there had been an accident and that her friend John Marshall was in hospital.

Corrie felt stunned. 'Is—is it bad? I mean, he will be all right, won't he?'

'He'll be fine,' the voice assured her, 'but he is asking for you.'

'I'll be there immediately,' she said, taking down the name of the hospital. 'Tell him I'm on my way.'

When she had put down the phone Corrie realised that there were all sorts of questions she ought to have asked. She had no idea what had happened or exactly what was wrong with him, but she knew without a shadow of doubt that her place now was at his side.

Her first thought was to phone for a taxi, but living as they did so far from any town it could be ages before one arrived. She would have to ask Damon if she could borrow the Rolls, an intimidating thought but not one on which she had time to dwell.

Gathering up her handbag and slipping into a coat, she almost ran along the corridor and arrived breathless, pushing open the study door without bothering to knock. 'It's John,' she said urgently to the two questioning faces turned towards her. 'He's had an accident. Can I borrow your car, Damon? They've taken him to hospital, in Dublin, I must go.'

'I'll take you,' came the short reply, adding drily, 'I don't want you wrecking my car in your haste to be at your lover's side.'

But in her present numbed state Corrie paid no heed to his taunt, conscious only that John was asking for her and she mustn't let him down.

Neither of them spoke on the way to the hospital, except when Damon asked her what had happened and she was compelled to reply that she knew nothing. All sorts of things were running through her mind, but for once her thoughts were not with the man at her side. At this precise moment he meant nothing to her; it was John who took her full attention. In a way it was all her fault, if she hadn't written him that letter he would never have come over and none of this would have happened.

By the time they reached the hospital she had worked herself up into quite a state and was hardly aware of Damon's hand on her arm, content to let him make the enquiries and guide her along to the ward into which John had been admitted.

She was shocked when she saw him. His head was swathed in bandages and his face ashen, except for several thin red lines across his cheek and a purpling bruise about one eye. The ward Sister touched him gently on the arm, saying, 'Mr Marshall, you have visitors.'

John's eyes opened slowly and when he saw Corrie he smiled. Licking dry lips, he said hoarsely, 'Darling, is it really you?'

Compassion welled up inside Corrie. He looked ghastly—and it was all her fault. 'Oh, John,' she cried, leaning over him and pressing her cheek gently to his. 'I came as quickly as I could. What happened?'

'A car came up behind me,' he said tiredly. 'I didn't hear it—I was thinking about you, and you know how quiet the roads are. I stepped out—next thing I was in here. You won't leave me? You will stay?'

His appeal caused tears to fill her eyes. 'For as long as you need me, my darling, you know that.'

He tried to hold her but was so weak that the effort exhausted him and he lay back against the pillows, breathing heavily, his eyes once again closed.

Damon had disappeared, though she hadn't noticed him go and she sat now, holding John's hand, talking softly, assuring him that he would soon be better and that she would be with him for as long as he needed her. She remained until the Sister came back to say it was time she left.

'He's asleep again now,' she said. 'There's nothing more you can do. He will rest easier now he's seen you and you can come again tomorrow.'

'How long will he have to stay here?' asked Corrie. 'Is it bad, his head? What's he done to it?'

'It was cut pretty badly,' said the nurse, 'and we can't be sure that there's no internal damage until we have the result of the x-rays.'

'But you're fairly confident that there's nothing else wrong?' persisted Corrie.

'I can't commit myself,' smiled the Sister sympathetically, 'but he's in good hands. He's your fiancé, isn't he? He loves you very much, your name was never off his lips when he was coming round from the anaesthetic. Aren't you lucky to have a man who thinks so much of you?'

Corrie nodded, there was no point in telling the truth.

The next moment Damon's hand was on her arm, ushering her back the way they had come. 'I'm sorry about John,' he said, when they were in the car and driving out of the hospital grounds. 'You look pretty devastated, but I shouldn't worry too much, he'll soon recover.'

Although he had expressed concern his face was grim. There was no sympathetic smile which she expected, indeed hoped for. Cheerful company was what she needed right now, something to take her mind off John's accident which she was still convinced was all her fault.

'I hope so,' she said earnestly. 'I couldn't bear it if they find anything seriously wrong. You don't think they will, do you, Damon?'

'No,' he said tersely. 'I had a word with the doctor. His x-rays are okay, he'll be out in a few days.'

Corrie felt herself go limp with relief and smiled happily. 'Oh, I'm so glad, you have no idea what this means to me.'

'I think I have,' came the abrupt rejoinder.

She couldn't understand why he was so harsh and forbidding. Wasn't he pleased for her? But she couldn't ask what was wrong, his mood did not invite questions. Consequently there was uncomfortable silence between them on the hour-long journey back to

Hawksmoor, and Corrie was glad when it was all over.

His father was waiting, eager for news. Damon disappeared the moment they entered the house so she and Charles sat together in the kitchen, drinking tea.

She told him all she knew. 'Damon was in a strange mood, though,' she frowned. 'I couldn't weigh him up. You don't think he wishes that something worse had happened to John, do you? But no—' aghast with herself for even thinking such a thing, she added quickly, 'that's ridiculous. He might not like John, but he wouldn't wish that on him. I only wish I knew what was wrong.'

Charles looked thoughtful. 'Hasn't it occurred to you that he might be jealous?'

'Of whom?' asked Corrie, bewildered.

'Of John. Of the way you went rushing to him as though he was the only man in the world who mattered.'

'He does matter,' argued Corrie. 'He's still a very dear friend despite everything.'

'I think you gave the impression that he meant something more,' said Charles slowly, 'just when I thought I'd convinced my son that—' He faltered, looking embarrassed.

'Convinced him what?' asked Corrie suspiciously. 'I hope you haven't been talking about me, Charles. What I told you was in strict confidence, I thought you knew that.'

Charles caught her hand across the table, frowning slightly, and looking to her for understanding. 'It was only in your best interests. Unless someone interferes you two are going to get nowhere.'

Corrie pressed her hands to suddenly hot cheeks. 'How awful! Oh, Charles, how could you? What must Damon think?' She couldn't see him ever believing that she loved him, and even if he did, what good would it do? His own opinion of her was too clearly defined, he would never change.

'Perhaps you might be interested to hear his reaction?' He paused expectantly, looking not in the least repentant.

Corrie shrugged. 'What does it matter? He won't change. I should imagine he found the whole thing highly amusing and I wish you'd never told him, Charles, I really do.'

'He wasn't amused,' he said simply, 'not even faintly. Surprised, perhaps, and more readily prepared to listen than I thought he would be.'

'So,' returned Corrie, 'now he knows how I feel. Where does that get us, apart from making me distinctly uncomfortable?'

'He loves you, too.'

For a moment Corrie was too stunned to speak. She looked at Charles in utter amazement, feeling the colour drain from her face and her heart begin to pound so wildly it was almost painful. 'Don't joke with me,' she managed to whisper at last. 'It isn't funny.' Damon in love with her! It was ludicrous. No one had ever behaved less like a lover than he had; why, Charles had treated her with far more kindness.

'It's true,' he confirmed. 'He had just told me when you came dashing in to say John was in hospital.'

'And now he thinks that—that it's John I've loved all along? That would account for his attitude. Oh dear, Charles, what am I going to do?'

He smiled understandingly. 'There's only one solution, you'll have to tell him yourself how you feel. Explain about John, hold nothing back, and if I know Damon the next thing you'll be telling me is that your wedding day is fixed.'

'I couldn't,' she said, horrified. 'What if he denies that he loves me? I couldn't bear to make a fool of myself.'

'You owe it to yourself, my child. Your future happiness is at stake. Can you afford to risk that?'

She shook her head miserably.

'Then go now, before you have time to think about it. I heard him go into the sitting room.'

Corrie rose but still hesitated. It was the hardest thing she had ever had to do—but if she didn't, then she would lose whatever slim chance of happiness she had. She must do as Charles suggested, it was her one last hope.

'Good luck!' called Charles as she opened the door.

She would need it, she thought, walking slowly along the corridor. He was so confident that all would turn out well, but she herself was full of doubts. It seemed to her impossible that Damon could ever have said that he loved her. He had never lost any opportunity in voicing his opinions, and love had figured nowhere in his vocabulary. Their relationship had not even verged on friendship; so what could she possibly say now that would alter his beliefs?

For several long seconds she stood outside the door, her hand on the knob, reluctant to turn it and walk into the room. When the door suddenly opened and she found herself face to face with Damon all she could say was, 'Oh, are you going somewhere?'

'To bed,' he said abruptly. 'Did you want me?'

His face was forbidding and she murmured, 'Er—yes, I mean, no—it doesn't matter. Tomorrow will do.' When you're in a better mood, she added to herself. To attempt to tell a man she loved him when his face was a hard expressionless mask was as impossible as trying to make conversation with someone who did not speak your language. In fact it was exactly the same. There was no way she was going to be able to get through to him. Why on earth had she allowed Charles to persuade her to try?

When he caught her shoulders and propelled her into the room Corrie cried out in dismay. 'What are you doing? I said it could wait, it's nothing important.'

'Important enough for you to come and seek me out,' he said, 'so fire away.' He dropped into his favourite position on one of the armchairs, his leg draped over the side. There was a certain cool amusement in his dark eyes as he watched her.

Corrie felt the strength drain from her limbs and knew she could not go through with it. 'I-I—' she stuttered before collapsing on to the chair behind her. This was awful, far worse than she had imagined. What to say, how even to start?

'You've been talking to my father,' he said tersely. 'Have you perhaps been discussing me—and you?'

She nodded unhappily. 'I'm sorry, it was Charles' idea that I come here, I knew it was a waste of time. I'll go now, forget I ever came. G-goodnight, Damon.'

But she had not even risen from her chair before he was towering over her, one hand on her shoulder holding her down. His dark eyes mesmerised her as she looked up, there was something in their depths that she had not seen before. A softening, but perhaps more than that; a need for her understanding—a silent plea.

'My father is right, we should talk. It's not good to bottle up one's emotions. You want to tell me that—that it's John you've loved all along? And I expect you called my father everything for opening his mouth. His intentions were good, though, you can't blame him. I'm just sorry that—that he told you how I felt. It's put us both in an embarrassing situation.'

'Is it right, then, that you—that you—love me?' The last words were a mere whisper, an incredulous hope that it might after all be true.

He nodded, smiling grimly. 'You see, I'm a bigger fool than I thought I was—but I'm man enough to know when I've lost, so I wish you both the very best.' He held out his hand and Corrie took it, pulling herself up so that she faced him.

'Damon,' she husked, her eyes never

leaving his face, 'you've got it wrong, I don't love John—I love—you.'

The hand that held hers trembled slightly and his eyes narrowed. For several long seconds he looked at her as if trying to read whether she was telling him the truth, then he pulled her roughly to him, his lips seeking hers in a kiss savage in its intensity.

The next moment, though, he had thrust her away, saying harshly, 'But I saw you with John. He still loves you, he needs you—more than I do. Anyway, I'd probably regret it if I got involved with you. Perhaps you'd better go now before we both say or do something we'll wish we hadn't.'

He turned away, waiting for her to leave, but having gone this far Corrie knew there was no backing out. Damon loved her! That was all she needed to know.

'John knows how I feel about you,' she said, not venturing to touch him, but noting the way he tensed as she spoke. 'It's true, he does love me, but because of that he wants only my happiness, even if it means losing me to you.'

'He's said this to you?' Damon faced her, faint hope shining in his eyes.

Corrie nodded, smiling. 'We had a good talk last night. He agreed to stay on a while longer, merely to act as a buffer against you. You see I couldn't take much more of your constant insinuations.'

'Oh God, my darling, what have I been doing to you?' Damon pulled her again into his arms, kissing her as though he never wanted to stop. 'I'm sorry,' he said between kisses. 'I truly am. I've been an idiot. My father's told me so many times, but it was only tonight that I really believed him. I was going to come and see you, I was going to put everything straight, until you came in saying that John had had an accident. You looked ghastly and I decided then that it was John you still loved. I didn't want to take you to the hospital, it was like driving to my own funeral, but I couldn't let you drive the state you were in.

'And then, when I saw you two together—well, that finally convinced me. I think I could have killed myself. Darling, darling Corrie, how can you ever forgive me for being so beastly? What can I say to make up for the anguish I've caused?'

'Just tell me you love me,' she whispered. 'I don't want to hear anything else. The past is already forgotten.'

He did more than that. He also asked her to marry him.

This made Corrie truly happy, but there was still one thing that bothered her. 'I'd like to, more than anything else in the world,' she said, 'but it's Zelah. Aren't you afraid that I'll turn out like her?'

He shook his head emphatically. 'I've been a fool. I should have seen the difference straight away, but I was so convinced that two people who looked alike must naturally act alike that I refused to give you the benefit of the doubt. My father tried to tell me often enough, but I obstinately refused to believe him. I still hate Zelah, my darling, I hope you don't mind, though for your sake and my father's if she comes back I'll try not to show it.'

'I don't think I want to see her either,' said Corrie, 'even though indirectly she's the cause of bringing us together. If I hadn't been determined to find her—'

'You might have married John by now,' he interjected. 'You wouldn't have been happy, I'm sure of it.'

'I think I would,' she said slowly, 'because I would never have known that there was any other kind of love. We'd have been good friends and perfectly content—but with you it's different.'

'In what way?' he asked, a smile gentling his lips.

'We shall be friends—and lovers,' she said shyly.

'No more holding back?'

'None at all. I belong to you now, completely. I've never felt like this about anyone else, Damon. I didn't even know such feelings existed.'

'Nor me,' he said. 'We're truly lucky.' He crushed her to him yet again. 'Darling Corrie, I suppose we ought to go and tell my father, but I'm almost afraid to let you go in case it all turns out to be a dream.'

She raised her lips to his. 'It's no dream. I shall be with you for the rest of your life.'

Photoset, printed and bound in Great Britain by REDWOOD BURN LIMITED, Trowbridge, Wiltshire